BLACKOUT!

When Diana Callan was beaten to death, all the evidence suggested that her husband, former Green Beret Christopher Callan, was the killer. He had returned from Afghanistan and developed violent blackouts, during which he could remember nothing. But another suspect was in the frame and if Chris could provide enough evidence to prove his innocence the real murderer could be punished. However, that was easier said than done . . . especially while Chris was involved with the girlfriend of a psychotic hoodlum.

Books by Steve Hayes
and David Whitehead
in the Linford Mystery Library:

FERAL
DEAD END
FANATICS
KILLER SMILE
UNDER THE KNIFE
CAST A DEADLY SHADOW
TOMORROW, UTOPIA

By Steve Hayes:
A WOMAN TO DIE FOR

By David Whitehead:
THE FLUTTERING
SCARE TACTICS

STEVE HAYES
AND
DAVID WHITEHEAD

BLACKOUT!

Complete and Unabridged

LINFORD
Leicester

First published in Great Britain

First Linford Edition
published 2012

Names, characters and incidents in this book are
fictional, and any resemblance to actual events,
locales, organizations, or persons living or dead
is purely coincidental.

British Library CIP Data

Hayes, Steve.
  Blackout! - -
  (Linford mystery library)
  1. Suspense fiction.
  2. Large type books.
  I. Title II. Series III. Whitehead, David, 1958 –
  823.9'2–dc23

  ISBN 978–1–4448–1329–6

Published by
F. A. Thorpe (Publishing)
Anstey, Leicestershire

Set by Words & Graphics Ltd.
Anstey, Leicestershire
Printed and bound in Great Britain by
T. J. International Ltd., Padstow, Cornwall

This book is printed on acid-free paper.

This is for the two A's —
April Melanie Crocetti
and
Angie Lynn Palmer

1

The punks in the lovingly-restored Mustang convertible made no attempt to hide the fact that they were following the airport mini-bus. For one thing the Mustang was candy-apple red, so it was almost impossible to miss. For another, they were playing rap music at full volume to constantly remind the driver up ahead that they were right on his tail.

As he turned left onto I-105 W, the shuttle-bus driver, whose name-badge identified him as Max Egan, checked his rear-view mirror for the umpteenth time. Although it was difficult to be sure, he counted three occupants in the car, all bobbing their heads and snapping their fingers to the rhythm of the thumping music.

Doggedly he pushed on, left onto Crenshaw Boulevard, right onto W 120th Street, right again, this time onto Prairie Avenue, then another left, onto Imperial Highway.

The Mustang stayed with him every yard of the way.

It was a little after seven-thirty in the evening and the traffic was finally starting to thin out. If the punks in the Mustang wanted to overtake him, they had plenty of opportunity. But they made no move to do so.

Immediately behind him, Max heard his handful of elderly passengers complaining among themselves about young people today and how they had no consideration for anyone but themselves. They wouldn't come right out and admit it, but they were feeling intimidated by the punks in the Mustang, which was doubtless the punks' intention.

Max felt intimidated too, which was surprising because he didn't look like the kind of man who'd spook easily. In his middle-thirties and a little bulkier than his five-ten height would suggest, he was clean-shaven and wore his mouse-brown hair in a neat buzz-cut that hinted at previous military service.

Keeping his steady blue eyes on the road, he tried to ignore the punks and just get on with his job. But he was already starting to sweat, and chew worriedly at his bottom lip. For Max, these were not good signs.

He took the Century Boulevard exit, followed it with a right onto World Way, and there, on his right, was his destination; Los Angeles International Airport, marked out by its distinctive 'theme building' — a restaurant that looked more like a gigantic white flying saucer standing on four legs.

He felt some of the tension easing out of him, took a left and sent the mini-bus up a ramp and under a sign marked *DEPARTURES*.

The Mustang took the ramp as well.

Max pulled up to the curb outside Terminal Four, cleared his throat and called mechanically: 'American . . . America West . . . Sun Aire.'

Then he got out, slid open the side-panel door and allowed three passengers to climb down into the balmy July evening.

As he went to get their bags from the storage area of the white mini-bus with its distinctive, bright orange *OnTime* clock-face logo, he threw a seemingly casual glance off to his right. The Mustang, he saw, had slowed to a crawl about a hundred yards away.

Once they had their bags and had pressed tips into Max's hand, the passengers were on their way.

Next stop was the Bradley International Terminal. Only two passengers alighted this time. They frowned back at the Mustang and asked Max what the world was coming to. Max could only shrug noncommittally and wish them a happy vacation.

He made his final stop at United Airlines — the last of the upper-level terminals. Max's last two passengers, an elderly husband and wife in matching fluorescent green Hawaiian shirts, stepped down off the bus and Max got their bags for them. Goodbyes were exchanged and then they disappeared into the terminal and Max was left all alone.

Still trying to ignore the Mustang, he slid back behind the wheel, scooped up his clipboard and quickly checked off his trip-sheet. Then he took the evening's fare money, slipped it into a plain manila envelope, sealed it and tucked it under the board's metal clip.

Grabbing the two-way radio he said: 'This is one-eleven, Base. All departures safely tucked in. Heading down to arrivals. Over.'

And that was when they finally made their move.

The Mustang suddenly accelerated from a dead stop and squealed to a tire-smoking halt right across the bus's path. Before Max could hit the button that would close the door the punks quickly crowded into the bus. Dark-skinned, lean and muscular, none of them was more than nineteen. They all wore baggy cargo pants, skin-tight vests, bandanas with their gang colors tied tight around their heads.

The leader, who had a cast in one eye and the faint promise of a Fu Manchu moustache adorning his upper lip, was holding a gun in his left hand, sideways on, just like he'd seen in the movies. It was a black and silver Colt Mk IV, the weapon of choice for today's career robber. Like his companions, he was Puerto Rican.

'Get out, *sarambiche!*' he snarled.

His voice was high with tension and excitement, a very dangerous combination when mixed with a handgun.

'Do it, man! Do it!' snapped the second punk.

Max stared at them each in turn, then carefully slid out from behind the wheel with the clipboard still in one raised hand, and followed them back down onto the sidewalk. 'If you want the money,' he said quietly, 'here, take it. But don't point that gun at me.'

The lead punk cocked his head and frowned. 'Say *what, sarambiche?*'

Max was starting to shake, and drew in a long, slow breath in the hope that he might calm down before it was too late.

It didn't work.

It hardly ever worked.

'Don't . . . point . . . the . . . gun . . . at . . . me,' he repeated slowly.

The punk to his right, bigger than his friends, with the face born out of a thousand street brawls, said: 'You fuckin' crazy, sarambiche?'

His voice unsteady now, Max said: 'No. I just don't like guns pointed at me.'

Their leader grinned. A gold tooth flared in the amber streetlight. 'Maybe you prefer I shove it up yo' tight white ass?'

They all laughed.

Max was now trembling noticeably. He looked at the punks but saw only —

All hell breaking loose.

An irrigation ditch.

Dig in!

Christ, captain, where are they all coming from?

The question all but lost beneath a cacophony of mortar fire, static from the radio, the whine of rocket-propelled grenades —

Hell breaking loose . . .

And then, in rapid succession, the names of the fallen — of Richards and Poole, Nelson and Crane, Griffin, Bel-laver, Muñoz, Dunn —

'Man, look at the *sanamagan!*' said the third punk, grinning. 'He's shakin' so bad he gonna piss his *pants!*'

Max blinked several times in quick succession before he could struggle back from whatever nightmare had briefly claimed him, and looked at the three punks.

'You sad shit,' said their leader. 'Gimme the money.'

Again Max looked at them, this time as if he was seeing him for the first time — which, in his subtly altered state, he was.

Then —

Fast as thought he lashed out with the clipboard, swiping the corner hard across the lead punk's forehead and opening a deep cut there.

As blood cascaded down into the punk's eyes he stumbled backward, gasped and then screamed, the gun in his fist temporarily forgotten.

Not missing a beat, Max spun, rammed the clip-end of the board into the second punk's face and broke his nose with a snap like splintering bamboo.

The third punk tried to run.

Too late.

Max was on him almost at once, chopping at his neck with the edge of the board. The punk went up on his toes, seemed to sigh, then collapsed as if he'd been filleted.

Max stepped back, shaking violently now, and sucking down great, shuddering gulps of air as if his life depended on it.

In some deep, dark part of his mind he knew he'd blacked out again. *Again*. And knowing that, he automatically forced himself to do a very odd thing. He visualized —

— a winter scene, with snowflakes drifting slowly, silently to earth —

— a tropical island paradise with a resplendent magenta sunset dropping over a golden blue ocean —

— and, incongruously, a scene from *A Day at the Races;* Groucho Marx taking someone's pulse and saying: 'Either he's dead or my watch has stopped.'

Gradually the fugue began to fade and something like normality started filtering back in. His trembling slowed, the sweat dried against his flushed skin. And then . . .

And then he was all the way back, experiencing the kind of jolt you must get slipping back into yourself following an out-of-body experience.

Swallowing hard, he took stock. He had no memory of what had just taken place, but the way the punks lay scattered around him pretty much told the story. Two of them were moaning and trying to staunch the blood, the third was unconscious.

Max quickly crossed to the lead punk, bent and ripped the Colt from his hand. Because weapons had once been the tools of his trade he worked swiftly and efficiently, deftly removing the recoil spring plug, pulling loose the slide stop, taking the slide off the frame, plucking out the bushing, the recoil spring and finally the barrel. When the gun was completely disassembled, he tossed everything into a nearby trashcan.

That done, he finally looked around.

He'd been lucky — no one had witnessed the confrontation.

Wearily he dragged himself back into the bus. The blackout was over, but the rage that always accompanied it left him absolutely spent.

The anger was a curse he had found almost impossible to live with. Dr Berg, at the Veteran's Association hospital in Sawtelle, had taught him the self-hypnosis technique that always helped him snap out of his blackouts, but so far he hadn't found anything to stop Max from boiling over to begin with.

Max hated what had become of him, of the thing Afghanistan had turned him into. But he was powerless against it. All he could do was go with the flow, even when that flow took him to all the dark places he'd sooner not revisit.

He started the engine, backed up and drove around the stalled Mustang, which was still pumping out mindless, repetitive rap at full volume. He told himself it was going to be a long night.

At that point, however, he didn't know the half of it.

2

He stopped at one of the airport service stations and washed his face in the men's room. After that he felt better. When he stepped back out into the night there wasn't even the slightest tremor in him; his hands were surgeon-steady.

On his way back to the bus he glanced toward the street and noticed a Yellow Cab waiting at a red light. The girl in the back seat was leaning out the open window so she could scan the street behind them. She was in her late twenties, he judged, with short, butter-colored hair cut in a chopped, pixie-like style.

She turned then, as if sensing that she was being watched, and looked right back at him. She had pale skin, eyes of some indeterminate color that he thought might be gray, a cute button nose, pouty lips, a strong chin and jaw.

She was undoubtedly the best-looking

girl he'd seen in a long, long time.

And then the light turned green and the taxi drove her on toward the airport and out of his life.

He stood there for a while, watching the tail-lights shrink until the radio inside the mini-bus crackled. He leaned into the vehicle and grabbed the mike. 'One-eleven. Go ahead, Base.'

Vinnie Carroll's cigarette-roughened voice said: 'Yeah, one-eleven. United Airlines passenger claims he left his wallet in the back of your bus. Check and get back to me, will you?'

'Can do.'

United Airlines, he thought. That would be Mr. and Mrs. Hawaiian Shirt.

Max climbed into the bus and made a quick search of the seats they'd occupied. Almost immediately he found the passenger's wallet in the shadows beneath his seat, opened it and raised his eyebrows. Seven hundred bucks and counting.

He went back to the mike. 'This is one-eleven, Base, I have the wallet. About seven hundred dollars and change.'

'Whooeee!' said Vinnie. 'What say we

split it fifty-fifty, one-eleven?'

For the first time that evening Max smiled, albeit briefly. 'Now, you know as well as I do, Base, that we'd only squander it on cheap booze and hot chicks.'

At the other end of the mike Vinnie coughed. He was a heavy smoker and had been since he was fourteen. One of these days it was going to catch up with him; one day *soon*, by the sound of it. 'Ah well . . . ' he came back, feigning regret, 'I guess we'll just return it to its rightful owner, then.'

'I guess we will, at that.'

'Take it to Friendly Skies, one-eleven. Customer waiting. Over and out.'

When Max pulled up outside the Friendly Skies terminal he found the elderly couple in the matching Hawaiian shirts waiting anxiously for him. The man came shuffle-running toward him, panic finally giving way to relief when Max held the wallet above his head.

'You're a star, is what you are,' said the old man, taking the wallet when Max handed it over. 'You should only have good luck.'

'Thanks.'

Before he could say more, a sudden, echoing squeal of brakes derailed the conversation, and Max looked around just as a white Cadillac jerked to a halt half-on, half-off the curb a few yards ahead of him. A chauffeur who was slightly smaller than the ARCO Tower immediately sprang out from behind the wheel. As best he could, given his size, he hustled around to open the nearside rear passenger door. As soon as it was opened a short, slim rooster of a man leapt out and marched across the sidewalk to the terminal.

He walked with his narrow shoulders set back and his face pointed straight ahead. He wore an expensive white suit — Armani, by the cut — and his black American Apparel shirt was opened to the sternum. His hair was black, too, oiled to a fine gloss and swept back from his small, tanned, spiteful-looking face.

The driver lumbered after him into the terminal.

The show over, Mr. Hawaiian Shirt started back toward his wife, stopped as if he'd suddenly remembered something and then turned back. He stuffed some bills into Max's hand, smiled again and clapped him appreciatively on one shoulder.

Max waited until he and his wife were out of sight, then looked at the money the old man had given him.

Seven dollars.

One dollar for each hundred he'd returned.

He laughed. He didn't really see that he could do much else. It had already been one of those nights — sometimes he thought *every* damn' night was one of those nights — and if experience was anything to go by, there'd be more to come before he finished his shift.

Just as he climbed back into the bus the terminal doors crashed open and the cocky little rooster in the white suit came marching back out. His massive chauffeur came lumbering out right behind him, one hand holding a suitcase with a *Save the Whales* sticker on the side, the other folded around the arm of a slim blonde girl in blue jeans and an open-necked white blouse under a man's-style tweed jacket.

The same girl Max had seen in the Yellow Cab, earlier.

Max narrowed his blue eyes and went back to linger in the open bus doorway. The way she was trying to pull away from the big lug told Max she was obviously being taken from the terminal against her will. He heard the girl shouting: ' . . . let go of me, damn you! Nicky — make him stop it! Let go! Get your goddamn hands off me, Tony!'

The little guy in the white suit — Nicky — stopped without warning and wheeled around on the heels of his Gucci loafers so that all at once he was right in the girl's face.

'Then quit screwin' around an' get in the car!' he yelled.

'Not a chance!' she shot back. 'I told you, I'm not coming back!'

Without being aware of it, Max started chewing his bottom lip again.

Then Nicky reached the Cadillac, tore open the rear passenger door and stood aside while the chauffeur, Tony, more or less threw the girl inside. Nicky followed her in and slammed the door behind him. Tony got back in behind the wheel.

For just a moment then Max was torn between allowing himself to witness what amounted to a kidnapping and doing something about it. Then he let his breath out in a shudder . . . and flopped back behind the wheel.

Don't get involved. Life's simpler that way.

He started the bus and drove slowly around the Cadillac. The girl was still screaming something, though he couldn't make out what it was. His eyes strayed to the rear-view mirror as he passed and was just in time to see Nicky's silhouette move hard and fast as he slapped the girl across the face.

Max thought: *Ahh, shoot.*

He stopped the bus and backed up, *beep . . . beep . . . beep . . .* until he was almost bumper-to-bumper with the Caddy. By the time he'd switched off the ignition and jumped out, Tony had also got out and was doing a pretty good imitation of the Great Wall of China.

'Back off, asshole,' he growled as Max came toward him.

Up close he looked ever bigger, with a small head on vast, downward-sloping shoulders. His hair was dark and curly, his face swarthy and surprisingly good-looking but for the kind of heavy, pronounced jaw you normally associate with steroid-abuse.

Max put his palms up. 'Hey, take it easy . . .'

Like nearly all big men Tony was slow and ponderous. Without warning, Max dodged around him and tapped on Nicky's window before the chauffeur could turn even halfway around.

Nicky's window whirred down and he stuck his head out. Everything about him seemed belligerent and intense, like he took a perverse pleasure in collecting enemies.

He was about Max's age, middle-thirties, with close-set eyes that looked like the color of jet beneath the neon streetlights. His nose, with its constantly-flare nostrils, was small and sharp. His sour mouth was a narrow, almost lipless twist. He was tanned and fit and instantly detestable.

'Don't be a freakin' hero, man,' he warned.

'Last thing on my mind,' Max replied.

'Then climb back in your bus and get out of here!'

It was probably good advice. But Max knew he couldn't take it, not and still look himself in the mirror. So he crouched a little in order to see the blonde beside Nicky and said: 'How about it? You want to stay or come with me?'

Nicky answered for her. 'She stays,' he said. 'Now take a hike before you get hurt.'

The girl nodded. 'Do as he says,' she said anxiously. 'Please . . . '

'Answer my question first,' Max said stubbornly.

Nicky shook his head as if in pity, let his black eyes move to a spot just behind Max and said: 'Bounce him, Tony.'

It was exactly the order Tony had been hoping for. Even before Nicky finished speaking, he moved in and grabbed Max from behind.

Without turning, Max brought one heel up and back and slammed Tony squarely between the legs. The big man doubled over, sucking wind, and Max turned to face him, punched him hard in the left ear, and Tony went down like a demolished tenement.

Max turned back toward the limo just as Nicky started reaching into a compartment in his armrest. Before he could reach the gun he kept there, the girl suddenly threw herself across Nicky's lap and slammed the lid of the compartment down on Nicky's wrist.

He howled in pain.

As the girl started to get out of the car Nicky made a grab for her. Max called his name, and when Nicky looked around Max punched him a short, powerful jab right in the face, then grabbed him by the open shirtfront to stop him from collapsing back on the seat.

Nicky's eyes were already glazed and rolling like marbles. His nose was bleeding furiously.

Leaning forward, Max said: 'Better not stop here too long, pal. You're in a three-minute zone.'

He went around the back of the car

and helped the girl drag out her case. She watched him with mixed emotions, glad to have been rescued, afraid of the inevitable reprisals.

'I know you meant well,' she said, 'but you shouldn't have interfered.'

'Now she tells me,' Max replied. He looked around. 'Come on. I'll walk you to your gate.'

'I'm not going now,' she said.

'*What?*'

'Nicky saw my ticket, so he knows where I'm headed. He'd just follow and make life miserable for me there.'

He studied her. He didn't know much about Nicky, but he knew enough to know that she was probably right. 'Can you use a ride back to town?' he asked.

'Please.'

As they walked toward the mini-bus, Nicky stumbled out of the Cadillac. His face glistened with blood and snot and sweat and it was all he could do not to pass out.

'You're dead meat, asshole!' he bellowed after them.

'You hear me? *You're dead meat, bus-driver!*'

3

They got into the bus and the girl more or less flopped into the first passenger seat. 'He means what he says, you know.'

'He means it *now*,' Max replied, sliding in behind the wheel. 'Tomorrow morning he'll have cooled off.'

'Don't bet on it. Maybe if I went back and talked to him — '

'Bad idea,' he said, starting the engine. 'Just stay put.'

As they drove down and out of the airport he said: 'I'm Max, by the way. Max Egan.'

'I know.'

'You do?'

'I read your name-badge.'

'Ah. And you are . . . ?'

'Kate Winslow,' she said. And then, with an ironic snort: 'Pleased to meet you, Max.'

He examined her in the rear-view mirror. He'd been right — she was in her late twenties, petite but athletically-built, with a mop of short yellow hair and large, smoke-gray eyes. She had clear, pale skin, a pert nose, strong white teeth and full lips.

As damsels in distress went, she scored a perfect ten.

'Where we headed?' he asked.

She shook her head, her mood sinking now as reaction set in. 'I don't know. I can't go back to my condo. It's only a block from Nicky's, and it's the first place he'll look.'

'How about a friend's place? Or a hotel?'

'Hotel, I guess,' she decided. 'But you choose. Nicky knows all my hangouts.'

As LAX fell behind them he felt her eyes on the back of his neck. At last she said: 'You handle yourself pretty well for a bus-driver.'

'What can I tell you? It's a jungle out there, lady. The octogenarians are the worst.'

She smiled, more from reflex than anything else. But her mind was still elsewhere. 'You better believe me, Max.

Nicky's not going to forget this. *Or* you.'

He knew it was true. 'Guess I'd better make a stop along the way, then.'

He pointed them toward Venice, but not funky Venice, just plain seedy Venice.

'What's the story with you and Nicky, anyway?' he asked.

'A long one,' she replied, and said no more.

It wasn't really long, of course, but it was one that gave her no pleasure to recount. Nicky had come along just after her boyfriend of eighteen months had dumped her, right out of the blue — for another guy. She hadn't seen it coming, hadn't even *guessed* that Rob was bisexual, and the shock had left her reeling.

When Nicky swaggered into her life all she knew was that she was hurting and she was vulnerable. He'd been crazy about her and made no secret of it, and she'd encouraged him because all that attention was good for her shattered ego.

It was only later that she realized he was a thug by profession, a leg-breaker who enjoyed his work a little too much.

By then she was his property, trapped in a violent relationship that made her feel even worse than she had before she'd met him.

All at once she felt the energy drain from her. She'd been planning her escape for weeks now; it was practically the only thing that had kept her sane. Now she realized that Nicky had probably known about it even before she did. All that time he'd been watching her, having her tailed, paying to have her computer hacked so that he could scan her browsing history and confirm what he already suspected. And his *pièce de résistance* was to let her to come within a whisker of making her escape — only to stop her at the last minute to make sure he crushed her once and for all.

Suddenly Max braked outside a run-down two-story apartment house.

'This is where you live?' Kate asked, grimacing.

'Home sweet home comes in all shapes and sizes, you know,' he replied.

'I didn't mean to judge.'

'And I didn't mean to preach,' he

countered. 'So I guess that makes us even, right?' He stood up. 'I'll only be a minute. Keep all the doors locked.'

She took one look at the squalid neighborhood beyond the window and then threw him a look that said: *Like I need telling*.

He let himself into the building, took the worn wooden stairs two at a time and let himself silently into his room.

He switched on the bare electric light. There was nothing homely about the place; it had never really been anything more than just a stopping-off point. No two items of junk furniture matched. A kitchen table with only three legs rested crookedly against the window sill for support. The most valuable item in the room was probably the old, battered portable TV on the coffee table in the corner, and even that had the dial knob missing.

Max went straight to the chest of drawers beside the unmade bed and slid the bottom drawer out. He reached into the space it had occupied and removed the .45 automatic that was taped to the bottom of the drawer above. He made sure the gun was loaded, then tucked it behind his belt, where it would be hidden by his blue uniform jacket.

He replaced the drawer, then rummaged through it until he found the other thing he'd come to get. It was a small, circular disc no bigger than his thumb-nail, made out of soft, semi-transparent plastic.

Gently he squeezed it. It made a soft, plaintive squeak of sound that wasn't unlike the meow of a cat or the cry of a baby.

Finally he went to the kitchen drawer, took out a short screwdriver and left the room.

Halfway down the stairs he stopped, checked to make sure no one was around, then knelt and used the screwdriver to pry one of the treads away from the riser immediately beneath it. Carefully he wedged the little squeaker into the gap so that it fit snugly. When he removed the screwdriver and the stair settled back into place, the squeaker was impossible to see.

Returning to the bus, he drove Kate through the night-dark city to a clean but

28

inexpensive-looking hotel in Santa Monica. Though she didn't know why, she felt curiously sad when the journey finally came to an end.

'How much do I owe you?' she asked, getting up and coming to stand beside him at the wheel.

'Regular fare,' he replied. 'Twenty-one-fifty.'

She counted out three tens and handed them to him. 'I wish I could afford more.'

'Forget it. This is plenty.'

She peered through the window at the hotel. 'Well,' she muttered reluctantly, 'I guess I'd, ah, better go in, then.'

'I guess you had,' he agreed.

She looked at him for a moment, then said: 'You're a nice guy, Max Egan.' Impulsively she leaned across and planted a kiss on his cheek. She smelled of some clean, fresh citrusy perfume, and after the shitty kind of evening he'd had it felt extra good in his nostrils. 'Goodbye . . . and thanks for everything.'

He watched her disappear into the hotel and felt a similar, illogical, inexplicable sense of loss.

Then the radio squawked, breaking the mood. 'Hey, one-eleven. You there?'

Max scooped up the mike. 'Here, Base. What you got for me?'

'Nothing. But I thought I'd better let you know. There's been some kinda screw-up with your social security number.'

'Screw-up?'

'Yeah,' Vinnie replied around another wet cough. 'Payroll says there's no such number.'

Max forced a grin into his tone that belied his growing unease. 'Mean I don't exist? That's a break.'

'Tell me about it. Can you confirm your number for me?'

'Sure.'

Once again he gave the phony number he'd memorized.

'That's what I got,' said Vinnie. 'Must've written it down wrong. Thanks.'

'Any time,' Max replied with a lightness he didn't feel. 'See you tomorrow night so we can do it all over again. Over and out.'

He slowly replaced the handset in its cradle and thought bleakly: *Looks like it's time to move on again.*

And for a man whose badge said his name was *Max,* he did a very strange thing.

As he thought the thought he called himself *Chris.*

4

From the bathroom of his penthouse suite overlooking the busy urban sprawl of West Hollywood and Beverly Hills, Nicky Crocetti took the towel away from his busted nose and inspected the blood it had blotted up.

The dark, crimson splotch only increased his fury.

Marching out into the living room, his steps making hardly any sound on the expensive Fereghan rug underfoot, he said nasally: 'I want that cocksucker, you hear? Get over to where he works, get his address, go there and find out where he took Kate.'

Anxious for a little payback of his own, Tony, his driver, nodded ponderously. 'You got it.'

'How bad you want him busted up, Mr Crocetti?' asked the third man in the room.

Like Tony, Bruno Corbucci was

immaculately dressed in black and heavily into bodybuilding. He was short and wide, with a dusting of dark, close-cropped hair around a shiny bald patch, and a jaw that was accentuated by a painstakingly-defined pencil-thin line of designer stubble.

Nicky stopped pacing so fast it was as if someone had hit his own personal *Pause* button. He stared at Bruno for a long moment, the towel pressed back to his nose, then said: 'So he never forgets me. And when I find that ungrateful, no-good *sticchio* I'm gonna make *her* sorry she was ever born.'

Tony shuffled uncomfortably. 'Better go easy on her, Nick,' he warned. 'Your ol' man won't like it if — '

Nicky whirled on him. 'Shut the fuck up an' get outta here!' he raged. 'You got a job to do, don't you?'

Knowing it was useless to try reasoning with him when he was in this kind of mood, they went.

★   ★   ★

It was simplicity itself to find out where Max lived.

He drove for *OnTime*. And after they'd roughed up the overweight sixty-year old dispatcher at the *OnTime* call center in Hawthorne, he couldn't give them Max's address fast enough.

'We're goin' now,' said Tony, towering over him. 'But don't you call an' tell him we're comin', Pops, 'cause then we'd have to come back an' start breakin' things you'd sooner not have broken.'

'Don't worry,' Vinnie Carroll replied, using the back of one liver-spotted hand to swipe blood off his mouth. 'The guy's not on the phone.'

He hated himself for having let these creeps walk all over him, but there hadn't been a whole lot he could do to stop them. He'd hated that he'd given out Max's address, too, but he was only human, and after the first couple of punches there hadn't been much he could about that, either.

'An' don't even *think* about callin' the cops,' added Bruno. 'You try to bring the cops down on us and I personally will rip your head off an' make it bounce.'

Vinnie stared up at him through wide, scared eyes. Before he could form a reply he was seized by another coughing fit. His face screwed up and his skin went red. All he could do was nod. *Okay, okay, I got it.*

★   ★   ★

Twenty minutes later Tony and Bruno drove slowly past Max's apartment house, which was in darkness, and parked around the corner. They walked back and let themselves inside, then took the stairs to the second floor.

They got halfway up when one of them hit the step beneath which Max had earlier wedged the small plastic squeaker. They froze as an indistinct sound filled the silence. Tony looked at Bruno. Bruno shrugged. It could have been a cat meowing, could have been a baby crying.

They kept climbing.

But the sound was all Max needed to hear to bring him up off the bed where he'd been dozing.

Having reached the top of the stairs,

Nicky's two enforcers ghosted across to Max's door. Each man slipped a handgun smoothly from under his jacket. Tony's fist dwarfed his matt black 9mm Smith & Wesson. Bruno's weapon of a choice was a Ruger SR9 that was roughly about the same size.

The two men looked at each other. Tony grinned. Then —

He shouldered the door. It offered negligible resistance and shuddered inwards. Tony and Bruno followed it in, drew up sharp when Bruno slapped Tony on the shoulder and pointed toward the open window, where a threadbare lace curtain billowed sluggishly in a light breeze.

They hurried to the window. Tony shoved the table aside. Since it now only had *two* legs, it fell over and came to rest at a steep angle.

Tony stuck his head through the frame and looked out. There was no fire escape and it was too far to jump.

Which must mean —

As Tony turned around Max came out of the shadows behind the door and whacked him across one shoulder with the missing third table-leg. As Tony crashed back against the wall Bruno twisted around and tried to bring his gun up. Max brought the table leg down on his wrist and broke both. The gun dropped heavily to floor.

As Bruno started howling Tony surged up out of his crouch, fighting mad. He slammed into Max and sent them both staggering back across the room.

They came up hard against the opposite wall, and Tony crowded Max and punched him wrist-deep in the belly. Max felt lights pop in his skull. His air left him in a rush and he sank down to his knees.

Tony hit him again and this time he stayed hit. The room turned, tilted and swam in and out of focus. Then he felt Tony grab him by his face and rasp: 'Get up, soldier.'

It was the last thing Max wanted to do, but he did it anyway, thinking about the Colt in his waistband and whether or not making a grab for it would only make this thing worse.

'Where'd you drop the girl?' asked Tony.

'Wh . . . what girl?' Max replied.

'The girl that's makin' your brains ring,' said Tony, and he clapped both hands at once over Max's ears.

The pain was beyond description.

Max groaned and tried to fold in on himself. He managed: 'Wish . . . I could . . . remember.'

Tony hit him with a roundhouse right that dropped him back to his knees. 'That help your memory any?'

Max groaned.

'I'll remember . . . *you* . . . that's for sure,' he grated.

'She ain't worth the pain, soldier,' said Tony.

'I'm . . . beginning to . . . realize that.'

'So tell us where you took her.'

'What . . . what're you . . . going to do with her?'

'That ain't your concern,' growled Tony. 'Your only interest should be stayin' alive.'

Bruno came over, the floorboards groaning beneath his weight. 'I gotta get this freakin' wrist fixed,' he told Tony, and kicked Max in the thigh.

Max winced, said breathlessly: 'I don't know where she . . . went. I took her so . . . so far and then she . . . told me to stop and . . . let her off.'

'You're lyin',' said Tony.

He hauled Max back to his feet and hit him in the stomach. Max fell forward and Bruno kneed him in the face. The blow shoved him upright again. Tony punched him in the jaw and Max slid down the wall, eyes shut, barely conscious.

'Better tell us, soldier,' said Tony, and someplace deep down Max knew he better had.

He said the first thing that came into his mind. 'Cumberland . . . Marquis.' It was a hotel in Mira Loma, about an hour's drive from where he'd actually dropped her in Santa Monica. 'But . . . I . . . I didn't see her . . . go in. So — '

Tony stared at him for a while, considering. The guy sure *sounded* convincing this time. He decided to give Max the benefit of the doubt.

Without warning he kicked Max in the head . . . and Max knew no more.

5

Kate spent a sleepless night in her Santa Monica hotel room, and when the sun finally came up on a new day it found her taking stock of her situation.

It didn't take long.

She had barely enough cash money to pay for the room. And if she knew Nicky, he'd already have had his people cancel all her credit cards. All she had to her name now was her luggage, her useless airplane ticket . . . and her jewelry.

Impulsively she unclipped the gold earrings and took off the diamond tennis bracelet. They'd cost Nicky an arm and a leg — somebody *else's* arm and leg, anyway. Even a fraction of what they were worth would be enough to set her up for a while.

She dragged the local phone book off the bedside cabinet and started searching for pawnbrokers.

Shortly after the stores opened at nine,

she was watching a short, overtly gay man in his late fifties, who owned *Pawn to Queen* on the corner of Ninth and Colorado, examine her items under a loop.

The store was a small, one-man operation packed solid with wall to wall junk. Kate felt uneasy in such an alien environment, but kept telling herself that the end justified the means — especially if the end, in this case, meant that she could walk out of this dump with enough money to buy herself a new ticket to anonymity.

At last the pawnbroker looked up at her. He was built like a jockey, almost the size of a boy, with a pinched, orange-tanned face and shoulder-length hair that was too completely chestnut for a man of his age.

'This stuff, hon,' he said, weighing the bracelet in his palm, 'it's not *hot*, is it?'

Immediately she bridled. 'Do I look like a thief?'

'I don't know,' he countered, fluttering his eyelashes beguilingly. 'What's a thief look like?' He offered a smile to take the sting out of his reply, then said: 'No offense, apricot, but I'll have to check this out.'

'Sure.'

He turned away, and swinging his narrow hips went through a plush red velvet curtain and into a back room. With no choice in the matter Kate drew a breath and waited.

And waited.

In the end it seemed to her that the guy was gone so long she suddenly found herself wondering whether or not he was planning to rip her off. Already paranoid and alarmed by the thought, she quickly snuck around the counter and up to the curtained doorway.

Even before she got there she heard him speaking softly into a phone.

' . . . oh yes, it's definitely her, Mr Crocetti . . . yeah, just like you said she might be . . . '

Kate froze.

There was an angry-bee sound from the other end of the line — Nicky. And she could just imagine what he was saying. *Figures. I knew she'd try pawnin' her stuff sooner rather than later, the stupid bitch.*

The pawnbroker's voice jarred her back to the reality of her situation.

'What do you want me to do, then, Mr Crocetti?'

She could guess the response to that, as well.

Stall her. Keep her there any way you can. I'm on my way.

She started to leave, remembered the jewelry, then thought: *Screw it. I need to get out of here* — now.

When the pawnbroker came hip-swinging back through the curtain twenty seconds later, she was gone.

★   ★   ★

At just about the same moment, in his private practice in one of Century City's more sumptuous high-rises, Dr Aaron Berg zipped his fly and decided it was almost a shame that he'd enjoyed this particular patient for the last time.

The girl who was even now slowly getting dressed was exceptionally gorgeous. Her name was Carol Frost and she was an up-and-coming young actress. But

43

like nearly all up-and-coming young actresses she was insecure in the extreme and in need of almost constant reassurance.

Dr Berg — a tall, spare, distinguished-looking man in his forties, who exuded charm and inspired trust — offered that in spades. And his bedside manner, as nearly all of his more attractive patients discovered sooner or later, was insatiable.

Berg went into his personal bathroom and straightened his tie. His thick, black-starting-to-gray hair had spilled down across his forehead. Now he finger-brushed it back, stroked at his neat, graying beard and plucked his glasses from his shirt pocket.

Outside, he heard Carol begin to weep and rolled his dark eyes before slipping the glasses on. It reminded him of that first time — she'd cried then, too, and frowning concernedly, he'd gone to her and said: 'Why the tears, Muffin? What's wrong?'

'I feel so ashamed,' she'd told him.

'About what?'

'What just happened.'

44

No surprise there, he'd thought. It was always their standard reaction, afterwards, and he knew exactly how to handle it.

'I thought it's what you wanted,' he said gently.

'It was, it was. And that's why I'm ashamed. I feel I've abused the trust you had in me.'

Berg had wrapped one beefy arm around the girl and squeezed affectionately. It had always been easy for him to feign affection. 'Nonsense,' he'd said comfortingly. 'You're too sweet to ever abuse anyone. You just wanted to share this experience with me. That's no crime. It's not even unusual.'

But that, he'd realized too late, was the wrong thing to say. She'd stiffened and pulled away from him. 'You mean, you and your other patients — ?'

'No, of course not,' he'd cut in hurriedly. 'You're the first and only one I've ever shared this kind of . . . closeness . . . with. What I meant was — it's not uncommon for a patient to feel sexually attracted to her psychiatrist.'

The girl was so gullible. 'It's *not?*' she

replied. 'Oh, I'm so glad. I need you so much, Aaron.'

And he had needed her, too — at first. She was every man's fantasy; a twenty year old, sun-bleached cheerleader blonde, with tanned skin and a perfectly-toned body. She wasn't very tall — he usually preferred women with longer legs — but she was still quite a prize, and he'd been delighted to add her to his long list of conquests.

'Now, no more tears and no more guilt trips, okay?' he'd said, and just like a puppy-dog she'd nodded dutifully. 'I'm your friend, Carol,' he'd assured her gently. 'And I'll always be here for you.'

But Carol had now outlived her usefulness.

She had been an enthusiastic and surprisingly proficient lover, and he'd had no complaints at all about the quality or the quantity of the sex they'd enjoyed during her so-called 'sessions.' It was only when she'd started making noises about *love* and *wanting to settle down* and *how they were so right for each other* that he decided the time had come to finish this thing — after one last 'session', that was.

He went back into the office and watched Carol's firm shoulders hitching in time to her sobs.

'You *do* understand how it is, don't you?' he said, as if it really mattered to him. 'You and I have shared something wonderful, Carol. It's been as special for me as I believe it's been for you. But I'm no good for you, not as anything other than a psychiatrist. You're young and vital, you have your whole life ahead of you. Me, I'm just a middle-aged man . . . and you deserve so much more.'

He was pleased with just how noble it sounded.

'But I don't *want* more,' she insisted, and he detected a hint of petulance in her tone that worried him slightly. 'I want *you*. We're *perfect* together.'

He shook his head. 'No, Muffin. You deserve much more.'

'So you don't want to see me again,' she accused with a pout.

'I want you to pick up your life again,' he corrected her. 'You're better now, cured. Ready to go back out into the

47

world and start auditioning again. Your big break's just around the corner, Muffin. How could I stand in your way, knowing that?'

'But I *love* you, Aaron.'

God, it was all he could do not to cringe at the word.

'And I have feelings for you, too,' he replied vaguely. 'But I have to remember that my job was not to give in to my heart, but to make you *well* again. And that job is done now.'

This routine had always worked for him in the past. All at once his patients would see him for the noble, selfless healthcare professional they believed him to be and no matter how upset they were when he ended their affairs, they always left feeling just privileged to have been a part of his life even for a short time.

But Carol wasn't about to go quietly.

'I'd give up my career like *that*,' she said, snapping her manicured fingers, 'so long as it meant we could be together.'

He turned away from her, deciding that the time had come for a reality check.

'And what do you suppose the APA

would do when it all came out that we had broken a sacred patient-doctor rule?' he asked. 'I'd be finished, Carol, *ruined*. You'd have sacrificed your career for a man whose own career had been ruined. Do you think we could live happily ever after on welfare?'

'As long as we had each other,' she said stubbornly.

'I'm sorry,' he said more firmly. 'It can never happen. We can't *allow* it to happen.'

'So you're dumping me,' she said miserably.

'You might think that now,' he said. 'But tomorrow, or next week, or next month . . . you'll see that what I really did was *liberate* you.'

God, he thought, *I'm good*.

But when he turned back and saw the light in her wide blue eyes flicker out, he realized for the first time that she wasn't just infatuated with him, as so many of her predecessors had been — this girl really *meant* it. She *did* love him.

'You'd better go now,' he said, shaken by the revelation. 'But remember, Carol,

I'll never forget you.'

'I don't want to live without you,' she said in a small, helpless voice.

'But you will,' he said, 'and the higher you climb, the more successful you become, the prouder I'll be of you.'

She seemed to realize, with that, that further argument was futile. Her head dropped and she nodded.

'Goodbye, Aaron,' she said.

Berg watched her leave and sighed. Why were even the difficult ones always so easy to manipulate in the end? Or was it just him — that he had somehow been born with an ability to tell them exactly what they wanted to hear and convince them that he was exactly what they wanted to screw?

He inclined toward the latter — it was more flattering.

The phone rang. Berg snatched it up, said: 'You know better than to inter-rupt — '

'It's your wife, doctor,' said his receptionist. 'I have her on the other line. She says she's on her way over.'

'Stop her,' he replied after a moment.

'Tell her I've gone to the VA hospital in Sawtelle — and not to call me there.'

* * *

Seated behind the wheel of her Mercedes S-Class 550 Sedan in the garage underneath Dr Berg's building, his wife Elizabeth listened as her husband's receptionist passed his message on.

'I see,' said Elizabeth.

She was an elegant, well-dressed woman of forty, with shoulder-length chestnut-red hair and sad green eyes. Her eyes right now were focused on a gleaming Jaguar XJS parked in a slot marked clearly with the legend: *DR A BERG*.

Next to it was a sports car with vanity plates that read: *4 C4R0L*.

'Did he say how long he'd be there?' Elizabeth asked casually.

'No, Mrs Berg. But I'll leave word for him to call you. So I'm sure you'll hear from him soon.'

'I'm sure I will,' Elizabeth said. 'Thank you, Alicia.'

She ended the call and got out of the car. The garage was silent but for the click-clack of her heels as she walked slowly across to her husband's Jaguar.

When she reached the car she glanced around as casually as she could. The parking attendants were nowhere in sight.

Good.

Taking out her car keys, she scraped, with great relish, the words *SCREW YOU* across the driver's door.

6

Max regained consciousness a little after dawn. He forced his eyes open, realized the room was really a blender going flat-out and dry-heaved until he felt better.

Better, of course, was a relative term. He was in better shape than, say, a corpse; but not by much. He sat up slowly, every muscle protesting, and cautiously checked himself over. Vision — okay. Teeth — all present and accounted for. No broken bones, but a couple of cracked ribs he might want to favor for a few days.

He looked around the apartment. He didn't think it could get any worse but Tony and the goon with him had surprised him. They'd trashed the place just for the hell of it and they'd made a pretty thorough job of it.

Well, it was no great loss. He was figuring to move on, anyway.

With infinite care he rolled onto all

fours and then used an overturned chair to help him climb to his feet. He had to wait then, until his stomach stopped churning and the rubbery floor solidified again. Then he went into the bathroom, ran a towel under the cold tap and set about cleaning himself up.

His reflection in the speckled mirror showed him the full extent of the job Tony and friend had done on him. He spat blood into the sink and then started unbuttoning his shirt. A hot shower should help.

It did. The needling water chased some of the aches away and after a time he felt himself loosening up, albeit slowly. He stayed under the showerhead until his head finally started to clear and he felt close to human again.

He was just easing himself into a pair of old jeans when he heard a distant sound that could have been the meow of a cat or the cry of a baby.

At once he froze.

A few moments later someone knocked at the door.

He shuffled over to it and said warily: 'Who is it?'

'It's me,' said a voice outside. 'Kate Winslow. Remember? You helped me at the airport last night.'

He made no reply.

'It's all right,' she said. 'I'm alone.'

He sighed. The smart thing would be to tell her to go away, that she'd already bought him enough grief as it was. But though he'd been many things in his time, *smart* hadn't always been one of them.

'What do you want?' he asked, forcing his mashed lips to make the question coherent.

'I . . . uh . . . may I come in?'

He sighed and opened the door. 'I hope this is important.'

The expression on her face slackened as she got her first good look at him, and she quickly set her suitcase down. 'Oh my God,' she choked. 'They found you, didn't they?'

'Long enough to do a little Fred Astaire on me,' he replied.

'I'm so sorry,' she said, sounding close to tears.

He turned away from her and limped

back to the bed, making every move as careful as he could. 'Thanks for the sympathy,' he muttered over one shoulder. 'How come you left the hotel?'

She closed the door behind her. 'I tried to hock a bracelet. The pawnbroker somehow knew it had come from Nicky, and called him.'

'Smart boy, that Nicky.'

'I was afraid to stay at the hotel after that, and . . . well, I walked around for a while, then — '

' — then remembered good ol' soft-hearted Max,' he finished, finally — and with some justification — starting to feel sorry for himself. 'Friend of waifs, strays and the poor, huddled masses.'

'I tried to find your name in the phone book,' she said, her voice small. 'But you're not listed.'

'What can I tell you?' he asked. 'I was getting too many calls from the White House.'

She cocked her head at him. 'Is it me, or were you nicer at the airport?'

'I had my work-face on then.'

'And without it, you're a royal shit,' she

said. 'Is that what I'm supposed to believe?'

'I don't know about the 'royal' part . . . '

Abruptly she reached a decision and said: 'I'm sorry. I shouldn't have come.'

He watched her pick up her case and go back to the door, then heard himself say: 'Wait.'

She looked back at him.

'I'm sorry,' he said. 'It was a rough night.'

She grimaced. 'For both of us.'

He glanced around. 'Listen, I've got a bottle of cheap bourbon around here someplace. Tastes better when you share it with someone.'

She shrugged and set her case down again. 'Considering my alternatives, I'd be a fool not to accept.'

He poured and then sat on the edge of the bed while she examined the full extent of his injuries. Eventually she went to his bathroom cabinet, helped herself to some bandages and salve and came back to do what she could to patch him up. He offered no resistance. In fact a part of him kind of enjoyed the attention.

His eyes fell to the *Save the Whales* sticker on her case and he said: 'You one of those?'

'Got to make a stand somewhere,' she replied simply, following the line of his gaze. 'Besides, they always remind me of my Dad.'

'*Whales?*'

'He used to take me whale-watching when I was a kid.'

'Uhn . . . Sounds like a nice guy.'

'He was. Tough outside, sweet underneath. I miss him a lot.' She let a quirky smile pass briefly across her lips. 'You know, you kind of remind me of him.'

'I do?'

'Yeah. He had this saying: 'Don't complain, don't explain.' Pretty much summed up his life.'

'I like him already.'

'And he would've liked you.'

An awkward silence settled between them — awkward because of its peculiar, unexpected intimacy.

'Look, I shouldn't have come here,' she said. 'You've already suffered too much because of me.'

'Believe it or not, I'm glad you *did* come back,' he said, the bourbon finally relaxing him and loosening his tongue.

She studied him closely to make sure he wasn't joking. 'Why?'

He tried to shrug and then thought better of it. 'I don't know. 'Cause you've obviously had a rough time and you could use a break, I guess.'

'You sound like a man who knows what he's talking about.'

'I do. About the rough time, anyway.'

'But not about the break?'

'Not yet.'

'Well, don't count on getting it any time soon,' she reminded him. 'Things are only going to get worse before they get better.'

'Why?'

'You sent Nicky's boys chasing off in the wrong direction last night,' she reminded him. 'That means they'll be back.'

'I was planning on leaving town anyway,' he said.

'I wish it was that easy for me,' she replied. 'But I have the feeling I could immigrate to Australia and Nicky'd still find me, eventually.'

'Because you're the love of his life?'

'Because I'm his property. Leastways, that's how he sees it.'

'You know, the more I hear about Nicky, the more I wonder how the hell you ended up with him.'

'How does anyone end up in any situation?' she countered. 'It just happens.'

'So what's your next move?' he asked.

'I get out of your life,' she said. 'I've already complicated it enough already.'

'I told you,' he said. 'I don't want you to do that.'

The bourbon had done something to her, too. She was silent for a long beat until she finally said: 'You know something? Neither do I.'

And she leaned forward and kissed him, very lightly, very gently, on the lips.

For a moment he almost forgot to breathe. Then he panicked a little, because he knew he should distance himself from this girl. His life was complicated enough as it was.

And yet there was something else about her, something he'd felt from the first, that in some strange way they were kindred spirits.

Even though he knew it was a mistake, even though it hurt his sore lips to do so, he kissed her again, harder this time. Then reason flooded back in and he came up for air and said: 'I think this is all getting away from us.'

She nodded. 'Do you *mind?*'

'That's the hell of it,' he said. 'I don't. I don't mind in the least. Right this minute I don't *care.*'

'Then hold me,' she said.

But still he held back. 'Maybe that's not such a good idea.'

'Why not?'

''Cause you've got a lousy taste in men, Kate Winslow. Nicky's a homicidal maniac, and me . . . '

'What about you?' she asked.

'I'm a murderer,' he said softly.

7

'At least I *think* I am,' he added.

'What does that mean?'

'It means . . . aw, forget it. Just forget I ever said it, and go.'

'No. I want to hear it.'

He took another drink. 'They say I killed my wife eight months ago,' he said tiredly. 'And maybe I did. I really don't know for sure.'

'Slow down, hoss,' she said. 'You're moving too fast. Let me hear it from the beginning.'

The beginning.

He sat there and thought: *Where* did *it begin?* But that was obvious.

It began in Afghanistan.

'Remember you said last night, about me handling myself pretty well for a bus-driver?'

She nodded.

'Before I went to work for *OnTime* 'Max Egan' was a Green Beret called

62

Christopher Callan. *Captain* Callan, if you please. And I did a tour in Afghanistan that turned out real bad.'

'What happened?'

'There were nine of us,' he said. 'Me and eight men, plus thirty Afghan soldiers. Our orders were to catch or kill a Taliban leader who was known to be operating in a part of the country just south of Kandahar. It should have been a pretty straightforward mission. It wasn't. Someone somewhere knew we were coming, and they were waiting for us.

'There were, I don't know, it seemed like a hundred of 'em,' he went on, losing himself in the memory now. 'Well-armed, well-supplied, well-trained. Just as we were entering this little village on the edge of a poppy-field we were going to torch on our way out, they came out of nowhere and opened up on us.

'That was usually the way they worked with the Taliban. Hit and run. Only this time they didn't run, they just kept hitting. All hell broke loose . . . '

All hell breaking loose . . .

' . . . and we had to fight our way out.

We lost our medic, Pfc Crane, almost immediately. My staff sergeant, Sergeant Muñoz, went next, hit by an RPG that also took out our communications.'

He looked at her suddenly. 'It was hell,' he said. 'I can't think of any other word to describe it. We got out of there fast. I spotted some kind of irrigation ditch and gave the order to — '

Dig in!

'We thought they'd call it a day after that, but still they didn't.

'I'd never seen the Taliban so . . . disciplined. They had mortars, RPGs, heavy machine-guns, the works, and they knew how to use them. They bombed the shit out of us. Then they launched a frontal assault.'

Christ, captain, where are they all coming from?

The question all but lost beneath a cacophony of mortar fire, static from the radio, the whine of rocket-propelled grenades —

'Five or six of our Afghans went down in the first attack. Corporal Dunn was hit by machine gun fire. I sent Poole and

Bellaver out with our heavy machine-gun in the hope that we might be able to outflank them . . . but they cut Poole and Bellaver down, not dead but wounded.

'They drew back then, the Taliban. Started taunting the Afghans, saying that because they were Muslims all they had to do was lay down their weapons and they could go free. All they wanted was us Americans, they said. Just lay down your weapons, hand over the Americans and then you can go.

'But the Afghans stayed firm. They knew that if the Taliban took us alive we'd end up having our executions posted on the internet.

'Even when the Taliban started shooting big, bleeding chunks out of Poole and Bellaver they stayed firm. Even when Poole and Bellaver started screaming for us to put them out of their misery they stayed firm.'

His voice broke, just once. Then:

'The day passed. I still don't really know how, but it did. And not once did the Taliban stop tormenting us with mortar and small arms fire. I thought that we might be able to make a break for it when the sun went down, but before that could happen, the Taliban charged us again.

'It was a massacre. I'd never seen so many of them.'

Christ, captain, where are they all coming from?

'I decided to make a run for the heavy machine-gun. If I could just reach it and thin 'em out a bit maybe we could still turn this thing around. The rest of the squad — what was left of them by then — gave me some covering fire and I made a zig-zagging run for it, but then something happened, I think a bullet hit the back of my helmet and knocked me out.

'When I came to it was over, and the Taliban had withdrawn. Every man who'd gone into that village with me was dead. Every man except me. And all I had was a headache. A lousy *headache!*'

His harsh laugh came out more like a sob.

'What happened after you got back to your own lines?' she asked gently.

He made another stab at shrugging and instantly regretted it. 'I submitted my report and faced a board of inquiry.'

'Why do I get the feeling they didn't buy your version of events?'

'They *did* — to a point. But I guess they thought I'd exaggerated the Taliban's numbers, training and weaponry to justify how so many men could have died during what should have been a routine mission. And let's face it, I wasn't the most credible witness. Thirty-eight men died and I walked away from it without a mark on me.'

'You got knocked out by a bullet.'

'Yeah, but the bullet hit my *helmet*. When I regained consciousness it was nowhere to be found.'

'So there was nothing to corroborate your version of events.'

'Precisely.'

'Oh, Max,' she said. 'I'm so sorry.'

He sighed. 'Well, that's where it began,' he said. 'After that I guess it started to tell on me — the way people looked at me, the rumors that started circulating about how I'd run out on my men. I started having nightmares — that's when I could sleep at *all* — and somewhere along the line I started having these . . . blackouts, as well. I'd get good and mad and afterwards I'd have no memory of what I'd done or why. So Uncle Sam sent me home.'

'To your wife,' she said.

He nodded. 'Diana,' he said. 'And that's where everything went from bad to worse.'

8

'We'd always had a great relationship until then,' he said. 'But now I was home all day, out of work, my army career was finished and I was undergoing psychiatric evaluation at the VA hospital. To say I was difficult to live with during that period is putting it mildly, and I guess I did more to push Diana away than I did to keep her. We argued all the time, or that's how it seems when I look back on it. And then one night we argued so bad that I could feel myself heading for another blackout.'

'What did you do?' she asked, her voice barely above a whisper.

'I got out of there, fast. I knew what I was capable of doing and so I went out, just walked around for an hour or so until it passed. At least that's what I *think* I did.'

'But you're not sure.'

'Not entirely. The next thing I remember is going home again . . . no, not going home, already *being* there, in the living

69

room, and seeing Diana . . . on the floor, bleeding. She'd been bludgeoned to death.'

'Christ. Were there any signs of forced entry? You know, like maybe a burglar had — '

'Nothing,' he said.

'So what happened?'

'Before I could call 911 the police arrived and arrested me. They said that someone had been passing our house and heard what sounded like someone being murdered, you know, screaming, hollering. But Diana and I never fought like that. We always kept it down.'

'Why?'

'Because of our daughter,' he said.

'You have a *child?*'

He nodded, and got up to retrieve his wallet from where he'd left it on the bedside cabinet. 'A girl. Ten years old. Her name's Melanie.'

He took out a photograph and passed it to her. It showed Kate a slim young girl with light brown hair cut into a three-quarter bob that fell in bangs around a pale face. The girl had fine brows, blue-green eyes, apple cheeks, a broad smile, slightly crooked teeth.

'And no matter how bad we fought,' Max continued, 'we never argued in front of her and even when she was in bed we were always careful not to raise our voices. Diana's folks had had a pretty bad relationship and she was sure it had screwed her up, so we were always careful to make sure the same thing never happened to Mellie.'

'But *someone* heard you fighting.'

'Someone *claimed* to hear us fighting.'

'Are you saying you were set up?'

'That was the impression my doctor got — the doctor who'd been looking after me at Sawtelle. He knew how violent I could get during my blackouts but he didn't think I could have committed murder. But he thought he knew who *did*.'

'Can you tell me?'

'Sure, why not? It was a guy called Eric Danvil, Diana's doctor.'

'What made him think it was Danvil?'

'If there'd really been the kind of fight that was so bad it made a passer-by call the cops, how come it didn't wake Mellie, who slept through the whole thing? The only reason we could come up with was that there was no such fight to begin with.

'So why did this witness, a woman named Lynn Yasuda, lie? We didn't know and couldn't guess, until Aaron — that's my doctor's name, Aaron Berg — discovered that she was one of Dr Danvil's patients as well.

'Coincidence? Aaron didn't think so. He wondered if maybe Diana and Danvil had been having some kind of affair behind my back — apparently Danvil had quite a reputation with some of his better-looking female patients — and that one or other of them had tried to finish it, they'd argued and he'd beaten her to death. The way Aaron explained it, it was at least a possibility. We just couldn't prove it.'

'But surely the police couldn't prove anything against you, either.'

'By the time the cops turned up I had Diana's blood all over me. And given my history of violent blackouts, I was a pretty solid suspect.'

'But . . . I mean, you're out now, free. They had to let you go eventually, right?

For lack of evidence.'

'Not exactly,' he said softly. 'I escaped before the case could come to trial.'

'*What?* How?'

'Let's just say I had a little help.'

'From Dr Berg?'

'You never heard that from me.'

'But hasn't that only made everything worse for you?'

'I don't know. Maybe. But it seemed like a good idea at the time. The idea was that if Danvil knew I was on the loose he might panic and do or say something to give himself away. Aaron's been trying to dig up something against him ever since I went on the run, but it's a slow process. Too damn' slow.'

Silence filled the room. He looked at her. 'So maybe it's not such a good idea after all, us sticking together,' he said.

She thought about that for a long time. He was probably right. He had his own problems, and she had hers. But he'd helped her the previous night — helped her and paid a hell of a price for it. The least she wanted to do now was help him in return.

'If the cops are busy looking for one man by himself,' she said slowly, 'a couple together . . . that might be good cover, take some of the heat off you.'

'Off *me*,' he agreed. 'But what about you? I'm not your only problem, Kate. You've still got Nicky to think about.'

'I know. And I think I've got a way to get him off our backs.'

He took another pull from what was left in the bottle and rinsed it around his sore mouth. 'I'm listening.'

'Nicky's father has a real soft spot for me,' she explained. 'Says I'm the daughter he always wanted. Maybe if I went and talked to him, explained how Nicky's been hassling me, he'd tell him to back off.'

Max frowned. 'You think Nicky would listen?'

'Definitely. He adores his dad. Besides, Papa Crocetti is the one with all the connections. Without his father's clout, Nicky's nothing more than a big mouth. What do you think?'

'It's worth a shot, I guess,' he agreed reluctantly. 'What the hell — go for it.'

9

Frank 'Papa' Crocetti lived in Fremont Place, an exclusive, gated estate populated by the rich and/or famous that was located in the mid-city area.

Max's battered Chevy looked just about as out of place as it could get in such opulent surroundings, but there was no point in getting embarrassed about it. Instead he allowed Kate to identify herself to security, then drove them through the gates and followed a spotless, elmshaded avenue until they came to a black-and-white, Tudor style mansion that was slightly smaller than Rhode Island.

The house sat at the end of a circular driveway, and was set amid vast, exquisitely-manicured grounds. Max parked a discreet distance away and stayed in the car while Kate got out and headed for the front door.

Two men in black suits immediately

descended the front steps to greet her. One was tall and thin, with black hair, an olive complexion and high cheekbones. The other was clearly hired muscle, big, bulky and intimidating.

Kate and the thinner of the two men spoke briefly. Then he escorted Kate inside while the other guy planted himself firmly in front of the door, his job obviously being to keep an eye on Max.

Once in the house Kate felt safe. Old-world serenity lived here, at least on the surface, and she had always enjoyed it. Not that she was under any illusions about Papa. As her escort showed her across a vaulted lobby toward a set of highly-polished mahogany doors and rapped smartly at one of the panels, she reminded herself that Papa was up to his fluffy white eyebrows in just about every dirty enterprise that would turn a dishonest buck.

But he was about as far removed from the stereotypical Mafia don as it was possible to get. Papa Crocetti had a certain gentility to him — at least when he was around Kate — and a sensitivity she found both surprising and gratifying.

'Come,' called a voice from inside the room.

Papa's Man Friday (it was one of Papa's favorite expressions, and it never failed to make him chuckle) was called Tomasino. He slid the doors open and allowed Kate to go inside ahead of him.

The room — it was decked out more like a workshop, really — was a shrine to longcase clocks and the clockmaker's art. It never failed to impress her, and today was no exception.

Papa Crocetti had always believed in indulging his passion for horology to the full, and over the years had acquired some of the finest examples of the clockmaker's art from all over the world. Grandfather clocks — longcases — were his special love, and there were more than sixty in the room, some built from cherry, others from satinwood, walnut or mahogany.

They stood side by side around the edges of the room, each one telling exactly the same time but ticking to a different beat from its neighbors. There were clocks from Belgium and France, clocks from Germany, Switzerland, Britain and beyond, and they nearly all had romantic names like *Morbier* and *Comtoise*, or *George III* and her own personal favorite, *Moonroller*. Some were relatively recent models; others went all the way back to the 1600s.

More than that, however, Papa loved to tinker with timepieces. Instead of a desk he had a long, cluttered workbench, over which he was even now hunched, inspecting some flawed example of jeweled movement through a neon-lit, goose-necked magnifying glass.

'Papa?' said Kate.

At the sound of her voice he twisted around on his stool, his thin, aristocratic face coming to life.

He was surprisingly small for a man who wielded so much power, and even more startlingly frail than the last time she'd seen him. He was heading towards eighty now, and had never enjoyed especially good health. He had a long face with loose, sallow skin, and benevolent, chocolate-brown eyes beneath the aforementioned fluffy white eyebrows. He wore a clipped white moustache and his bald head was dotted with liver spots, as were the backs of his vein-threaded hands.

He got up, put on a pair of gold wire-framed glasses and shuffled across to her, and they embraced gently and warmly. She said: 'I hope I'm not interrupting you, Papa.'

'You?' he replied. 'Never, Katarina.' His eyes travelled to Tomasino and he said: 'Two espressos, *daje!*'

Taking her by the hand, he led her to an overstuffed sofa where they sat side by side. He wore a comfortable pair of grey slacks and slippers, a white shirt open at his scrawny chicken-neck and a mustard-yellow cardigan. He looked so benevolent that it was almost impossible for her to believe that he could have fathered something as dark and sick as Nicky.

But it was only *almost* impossible.

She had known nothing about him until after their first meeting. Then she'd performed an internet search and discovered the truth — at least as much as was known — about Papa Crocetti.

He'd been born an only child in

Alcamo, Sicily, in 1937. His father had been killed in action during the Battle for Rome in 1944. In 1948 his widowed mother had brought him to America, where she had married a Jewish bandleader and he, 'Little Frankie', had been more or less allowed to run wild.

By the time he was seventeen Frankie Crocetti was the head of his first gang, whose crimes included extortion, theft and beer running. With typical Sicilian reserve he kept his operation small and largely anonymous, but when rival gangs attempted to infiltrate his territory in 1953 he added a number of so-called 'enforcers' to his private army and dealt permanently with his would-be competitors.

Although he personally detested violence, and as far as anyone knew had never taken part in or even witnessed any of the hits he had sanctioned, the short, violent war had taught Papa a lesson — that he had to expand or die.

And so he set about ruthlessly and systematically seizing control of all his neighboring territories.

There had followed a lengthy period of inter-gang warfare with heavy casualties on all sides. Eventually Papa called a meeting of the various factions and suggested it would be healthier all around if everyone simply swore allegiance to him. If they took care of him, he would take care of them, *capisce?*

Two gang-bosses refused in no uncertain terms and despite impressive security both men and their immediate families were shot dead within twenty-four hours.

The other bosses reconsidered Papa's suggestion and decided that maybe he had a point after all.

Papa's empire grew quickly from that day forward. He fostered and gained a reputation for fairness and diplomacy — but never would anyone describe him as a pushover. Any dissent was always quickly and permanently dealt with.

Now this sweet-looking old man said gently: 'How are you, Katarina?'

She wasn't sure if he knew why she was here or not. He had seemed genuinely surprised to see her. But with Papa Crocetti, of course, you never knew for sure.

'The truth?' she asked.

'Always the truth, child,' he replied. 'Time is too short to waste on lies.'

'Truthfully, then — no. I'm not happy at all.'

'Nicky?' It was more of a statement than a question. 'He is responsible for your unhappiness?'

'Yes, Papa. Though I guess I'm to blame too.'

'And you have come to me for help in this matter?'

She nodded.

'Then we will talk,' he said. 'And I will do whatever I can to make things right again.'

* * *

When the Chevy drove away thirty minutes later, Tomasino joined the big man at the front door and said: 'Put the word out, Sergio. Mr Crocetti wants to know who that guy is.'

* * *

'So,' said Max as he drove them back toward town. 'How did it go?'

'Papa's promised to talk to Nicky,' she replied. 'Make him understand that he doesn't own me, and can't keep me under lock and key.'

'That's a start.'

She nodded. 'I wanted to tell him I was never going to see Nicky again, but I didn't dare. The old man as much as said he'd only help me if I wasn't going to fly the coop.'

'When's 'Papa' giving you an answer, then?'

'Tomorrow. I'm to be here at noon.'

'Okay.'

She felt some of the tension leaving her for the first time since Nicky had dragged her screaming from the airport terminal. 'Thanks, Max,' she said, meaning it. 'I wish there was something I could do to repay you.'

He glanced at her. 'Me? What did *I* do?'

'Don't undersell yourself. You've given me hope — and I haven't had that in a long, long time.'

'Well,' he said hesitantly, 'there is *something* you could do for me.'

'Name it.'

He took a deep breath, and did.

10

The Sacred Heart Catholic Girls' School operated from out of an impressive old Spanish building. Kate stood at the decorative iron gates, watching as girls of all ages in smart blue-and-white uniforms trooped out for lunch.

Kate scanned the faces until she recognized a petite ten year-old with a pale face. She was a dead ringer for the girl in the photograph Max had shown her earlier.

As the girl passed through the gates Kate called: 'Melanie?'

The girl looked around, frowned at her. 'Hi,' she said warily. 'Who are you?'

'I'm Kate,' Kate replied. 'A friend of your daddy's.'

The girl's frown deepened, her pale, fine brows dropping lower over her large, blue-green eyes. 'Are you a reporter?' she asked.

Kate laughed and shook her head. 'Just a friend.'

Melanie perked up at that and came closer. 'Why didn't daddy come himself?' she asked.

'It's too risky,' Kate replied, sobering and dropping her voice a notch. 'He said the police might be watching you, and — '

'Where is he?' the girl interrupted.

'At a phone booth,' Kate replied. 'Waiting for you to call.'

The girl's smile seemed to brighten the whole day. Her slightly crooked teeth, Kate saw, were now caged behind a brace. 'Mean I can talk to him?'

'Sure can,' said Kate. 'There's a payphone around the corner. You can call him from there.'

'Can't I use my cell?'

'He doesn't think that's such a good idea, sweetheart. They might be monitoring your calls as well.'

That made sense. After a moment the girl nodded, and suddenly it was all Kate could do to keep up with Melanie as they set off for the booth.

★ ★ ★

Max was in a coffee shop two blocks away, waiting anxiously beside one of two payphones in an alcove outside the restrooms. The instant the phone rang, he snatched up the receiver.

'Max,' he said quickly.

'All clear,' said Kate, at the other end. 'I'll put her on.'

Max immediately felt his throat tighten. Suddenly the coffee shop, the comings and goings of its patrons and the background buzz of conversation they made, faded to nothing.

Then —

'Daddy? Is that you?'

He swallowed, blinked rapidly as his vision threatened to blur. 'It sure is, sweetheart,' he said thickly. 'God, it's great to hear your voice.'

'You too, daddy,' said Melanie. 'Where are you?'

'Not far, kitten. Listen, I want you to do me a great big favor.'

'What?'

'Let Kate bring you to see me.'

Silence.

Then: 'But Aunt Cora said I mustn't — '

87

'Never mind what your aunt says, sweetheart. Do it for me, will you?' When she made no reply he asked uncertainly: 'You *do* want to see me, don't you?'

'Yes.'

'Then go with Kate. She knows where to meet me.'

Melanie's continued silence unnerved him. He didn't want to sound desperate but he couldn't help it.

'It'll only take a few minutes, I promise. Please say you'll do it.'

'All right,' she said.

He sagged. 'Thank you, honey.'

He hung up, collected himself, then turned and started back out into the dining area — stopping abruptly when he saw two CHP officers enter then take the booth right beside the exit.

Fear hit him then like a smack in the mouth. He couldn't stay here and he couldn't leave without having to pass right by them. He swallowed again, felt himself starting to shake and knew that another blackout might be imminent.

No, he thought. *Please, God, not now.* Desperately he looked around. Even though he tried to keep them casual, he knew his movements were jerky, apt to draw unwelcome attention. He spotted a copy of the *LA Daily News* on the counter, snatched it up and then started toward the door, keeping his head down, pretending to read.

'*Hey, buddy!*'

The whole world suddenly seemed to stop revolving. Silence briefly claimed the coffee shop. The cops looked up from the menu. Max turned toward the man who'd called out to him.

The attendant behind the counter said: 'Where you goin' with my paper?'

Sweating noticeably now, Max refolded the paper and threw it back on the counter, where he'd found it. 'Sorry,' he managed in a strangled voice. 'I didn't know it belonged to anyone.'

He turned and continued on toward the exit.

From the corner of his eye he saw the cops looking at him, more curious than suspicious. He rubbed at one eye, hoping the gesture would cover his face as he went past them.

He stepped out onto the street, feeling weak in the legs. But he'd made it. Sucking down air, he walked away as casually as he could, fighting the urge to run.

* * *

In the coffee shop one of the cops said: 'Did that guy look familiar to you?'

The other cop shook his head. 'Want to check him out?'

Before the first cop could decide, a waitress came up to take their order. 'Hi guys. What'll it be?'

The second cop lifted one hand. 'Hold on a sec, Maggie.' And to his partner: 'Well? It's your call.'

The first cop thought for a moment, then shook his head. 'Screw it. Let's eat.'

* * *

Briarwood is what they call a small, grassy 'pocket park' with tree-lined walkways. On any given day at almost any given time between dawn and dusk you can guarantee to find it populated with joggers in designer sweats and nannies pushing fancy baby strollers.

By the time Max arrived Kate and Melanie were waiting for him on a concrete bench overlooking the modest picnic area. As soon as she spotted him Melanie jumped up and ran to meet him. Max dropped to one knee and hugged her as if he never wanted to let her go.

Mellie . . . Mellie . . . Mellie . . .

After a moment he got up, took Melanie's hand and led her toward the trees. It was safer there, not quite so public. They found a sun-dappled spot and sank down onto the grass, while Kate remained on the bench, keeping watch for them.

Max looked at his daughter, saw how much she'd grown, how much of her growing he'd missed out on. 'I've missed you so much, sweetheart,' he said.

Melanie was studying him, too, remembering him as he was and seeing him as he was now — thinner, wearier, sadder.

'Missed you too,' she managed. And then, unable to contain herself any longer, she threw herself at him again and said: 'Oh, daddy, when are you going to give yourself up?'

He was surprised by the question. 'Is that what you want me to do?'

She pushed away from him and nodded.

'But then I'll go to prison.'

'I know. But . . . well, at least I'll be able to see you then. Besides . . . '

'What?'

'Aunt Cora says it's the right thing to do.'

'I'll bet she does,' he muttered. Well, she would, wouldn't she? Like everyone else, she was convinced that he'd murdered her sister. 'What, ah . . . what else does she say about me?'

'Nothing much.'

'Does she still think I . . . I did that awful thing to mommy?'

Melanie looked very serious now. 'I don't know. We never talk about it. Except when something happens at school.'

'What do you mean?'

'You know,' she said uncomfortably. 'When kids say nasty things about you.

Call me bad names.'

Max felt his euphoria evaporating. 'There's a lot of that, is there?' he asked.

'Not too much. Not like before. You know . . . when it was on TV and in the papers and stuff. Then they did it all the time.'

He drew her to him again, more gently this time. 'I'm so sorry, kitten. It must be awful for you.'

She shrugged her small shoulders. 'It's not so bad,' she said. 'I don't believe them, no matter what they say. I know you didn't hurt mommy. You couldn't. You still loved her.'

That surprised him, and he tilted his head at her. 'Is that what Aunt Cora says?'

She shook her head. 'Uh huh. Mommy told me. Used to say it all the time. That's why I got mad at her sometimes. You know — for not loving you back.'

'Well, just so you always believe in me, that's all that matters,' he said.

★   ★   ★

He wished her lunch-break could have lasted for ever, or that everything would suddenly change so he could be just like a normal father, meeting his kid from school and spending quality time with her while she was still his little girl.

But that wasn't the way of it, and for all he knew it never would be. So fifteen minutes later they rejoined Kate and all three walked back to the Chevy, where Kate climbed in behind the wheel to give them one last moment of privacy together.

As they hugged Melanie whispered into his ear: 'Bye, daddy. Love you lots.'

'Me you too. A whole ton.'

Melanie climbed into the passenger seat and tugged the belt across her tiny frame. 'I won't forget,' she assured him. 'About this being our secret and everything.'

'I know you won't,' he said around the lump in his throat. 'See you soon, kitten. 'Bye.'

He had to force himself to let go of her hand, and as Kate drove her away his shoulders sagged, his head dropped and he did the best he could to stifle a sob that sounded like it contained all the sadness in the world.

11

'I don't see any of Nicky's men or cars around,' said Kate.

She'd dropped Melanie back at school, collected Max from Briarwood and then expressed a desire to go back to her condo to pick up some things. Max hadn't cared much for the idea, but had agreed to at least go check out the lay of the land.

Now they sat in the old Chevy, double-parked outside her apartment block on Wilshire Boulevard, and he had to admit, everything seemed okay.

'Want me to come up with you?' he asked.

She shook her head. 'Uh-huh. I just need to grab a few extra things, that's all. I'll be back in a sec.'

She got out of the car and he watched her hurry into the building. Still feeling uneasy, he pulled over and parked at the curb.

Kate took the elevator to her seventh-floor apartment, went directly to her door and let herself inside.

She froze.

The place looked as if a tornado had swept through it. The furniture had been tipped over, decorative bowls of colored beads had been spilled everywhere and her paintings had been ripped from the walls and slashed to shreds. Anything that could be smashed had been — lamps, mirrors, vases, everything.

A small, anguished moan escaped her.

She stumbled deeper into the room like a girl in a bad dream, not thinking to close the door behind her. No matter how much destruction she saw, she still couldn't believe that anyone could have done this to her place, her *home*, or that Nicky could have been so spiteful as to have ordered it done —

Oh God.

The bedroom was even worse.

The bed had been upended, the mattress ripped open. Paint-covered bed sheets were scattered everywhere like wounded ghosts. Someone had painted *BITCH* across the mirrored doors of her closet and when she finally summoned the courage to slide one closet door aside, she saw that every stitch of clothing she owned had been torn seam from seam.

No . . . no . . .

Emotion made her screw her face into the beginnings of a sob, but before she could submit to it she heard the softest sound behind her and then a deep voice said sociably: 'Welcome home, princess.'

★ ★ ★

'Let's make this quick,' said Nicky, looking across the desk at his visitor.

He was smoking a large cigar, more for effect than anything else. After all, image was everything in his business. Although first and foremost you had to get results, you also had to look the part — and so far, Nicky had managed to do both, to great financial success.

But the more he'd studied his reflection in the mirror that morning, the more he'd felt that his recently-broken nose added . . . character . . . to him. It was like a badge of honor. It said: *Yeah, I've been around. An' as you can see, I can take the knocks as well as hand them out.*

So he'd decided against getting it fixed. In his own mind, at least, it made him look tougher.

The tanned, sandy-haired man on the other side of the desk smiled at him. He was a young, well-groomed, clean-shaven lawyer named Ethan Perry, and he was Nicky's liaison with the legal firm that so often employed him, Messrs Patterson, Gimlin and Wallace.

'This won't take a minute,' Perry said amiably. 'Our office just wanted to thank you for helping us win the Rabanski case. If you hadn't dug up that, uh, 'cooperative' witness, we never would've even gone to trial.'

Nicky studied him through a cloud of fragrant blue cigar smoke, then shook his head in amused, thinly veiled contempt. 'Who the hell do you think you're talkin' to, Perry?' he finally asked.

'Excuse me?'

'You come in here, cordial as can be, actin' like you're all so grateful to me . . . but I hear what you an' your people *really* say about me around your conference tables. You hate my freakin' guts, all of you — '

Perry sat back. 'Oh now, come on, Nicky. That's not true — '

But Nicky had started. Nothing was going to stop him now, and Perry knew it.

'You wouldn't even be in the same *country* as me if I wasn't so goddamn valuable to you,' accused Nicky.

Perry sighed but didn't bother to deny it. They'd both know he was lying if he did.

His relationship with Nicky had always been fragile. In fact, he'd often likened dealing with Nicky to trying to defuse a bomb that never stopped ticking down to zero.

But Ethan Perry was nothing if not diplomatic. That was the reason he'd been given this job in the first place — because his bosses felt he, above all others, could take all the BS Nicky dished out and still smile agreeably at the end of it.

Still, every so often Nicky needed to be reminded just who was really in charge here, and Perry was adept at that, too. So now he replied easily: 'Oh, you're valuable, all right, Nick. Of course you are. But in fairness, we *do* pay you very handsomely for your, ah, services.'

'Hey, I ain't complainin' about the bucks,' said Nicky. 'And you know somethin'? I don't really give a rat's ass *how* you feel about me.' He leaned forward across the desk and blew smoke. 'Wanna know why?'

Perry didn't, but said: 'Go on.'

'Because it doesn't even come *close* to what I think of *you* cocksuckers,' Nicky gloated.

Perry smiled a little broader. 'I'll tell you what,' he said, trying to sound patient and reasonable. 'Why don't you just get whatever it is that's bothering you off your chest and then we'll get down to business?'

'All right,' said Nicky. 'You pay me 'cause I got heavy connections, right? 'Cause I don't mind gettin' my hands dirty an' I get the job done. An' that's *all* you pay me for. So let's cut all that *Thanks for helpin' us win the Rabanski case* crap and just get to the bottom line. Whose legs do you want me to break this time?'

Perry put his gray leather attaché case on his lap, opened it, took out a file folder and tossed it onto the desk. 'It's all in there, Nick,' he said, and got to his feet. 'Have a nice day.'

Nicky watched him go, then threw the cigar at the door after the lawyer had closed it behind him. 'Prick,' he muttered.

The phone rang. He let it ring for a while, his belligerent gaze still fixed on the closed door. At last he answered it, snapped: 'What is it?'

'Nicky?'

Nicky stiffened, softened his tone at once. 'Papa. Yeah, Papa, it's me.'

'You sound upset, Nicky,' the old man said gently.

'Ah, you know how it is.'

'I know there's been trouble with Kate.'

Nicky frowned, though there was no mystery to it. Papa knew more or less everything . . . but *only* more or less.

'She came to see me this morning, Nicky,' said Papa. '*She* was upset, too.'

'Don't sweat it, Papa. We had a little disagreement, that's all. She over-reacted.'

'It didn't seem that way to me, Nicky.'

'You know women.'

'I also know you got a temper, Nick. That you enjoy hurting people.'

'Not the people I *love*, Papa. Not Kate. Shit, I've treated her like a fuckin' princess.'

At the other end of the line Papa sucked in a sharp breath. 'Watch your mouth, Nicky,' he said. 'Words like that have no place in my life.'

'Sorry, Papa. It's just that it pisses me off when she tries to take advantage of your kindness to — '

'She's not taking advantage of me, Nicky,' Papa said patiently. 'She's *scared*. Whatever it is that's in you, it scares her. It scares *me*. I worry for you, son. And she worries for you, too.'

'I'm fine.'

'Listen, Nicky,' said Papa. 'You and me, we live in a different world to most other folks. Sometimes you got to employ force when all other means fail. It's a shame, but that's the way it is. But that doesn't mean you have to *enjoy* it.'

'Who says I enjoy it?'

'Nicky, Nicky, you *relish* it!' the old man said wretchedly. 'Show me a woman who *wouldn't* be scared of a man who enjoys the suffering of others the way you do.'

'Then what do you want me to do about it?' asked Nicky.

'I love Kate,' said his father. 'I want her for my daughter-in-law. So treat her good. Buy her flowers, perfume, clothes. Women love that kind of thing. Like your dear Momma used to say, sweetness opens more bedroom doors than a busted kneecap.'

A light flashed on the telephone console and Nicky said: 'Hold on, Papa. I got another call comin' in.' He switched lines and said: 'Talk to me.'

Tony said: 'We got her, Nick. Waltzed right in while we was, uh, rearranging the place.'

For the first time that morning Nicky smiled with genuine warmth. 'Beautiful

. . . No, sit tight, Tony. I'll be there soon as I can.'

'Got it.'

'Oh, an' Tony . . . '

'Yeah?'

'Show her what can happen when I'm not around to protect her, will you?'

12

Tony ended the call and slipped the cell phone back into his jacket pocket. When he turned back to Kate his expression was like marble — hard and cold. Without a word he crossed the room toward her. She tried to struggle but the man who'd helped him trash her place was now holding her from behind, making it impossible to break free.

She had recognized Tony's companion immediately, and his presence had chilled her blood. His name was Aristofani Arena, and he was the man Nicky always took with him on his 'special' jobs.

Arena was a massively fat man of about average height, with a black buzz-cut and pale green eyes. He was almost forty, had no discernible neck, wore a beard that was more stubble than anything else, and seemed incapable of closing his mouth. She couldn't remember a time when it hadn't hung slack on his jaw, giving him the impression that he was somehow retarded.

He wasn't. He was sharp and quick, but he loved to inflict and witness pain almost as much as Nicky, and that had created a special bond between them. She suspected that even Tony had a line beyond which he wouldn't or couldn't go. But for Aristofani Arena no such line had ever existed.

Now Tony looked down at her with an expression she'd never seen on him before. He slowly, brazenly inspected her from the tips of her toes to the top of her head, then smiled.

'I've often wondered about you, princess,' he said, and savoring every moment, started to unbutton her blouse.

Her eyes widened and she renewed her struggles. 'Are you nuts?' she asked. 'Nicky'll *kill* you for this.'

Tony's broad shoulders rose and fell. 'I'll take my chances.'

And not missing a beat he went right on unbuttoning her blouse.

Outside, Max was starting to wonder what was taking Kate so long. She'd only been gone for about ten minutes, but somehow they'd seemed more like ten hours, and all at once he was too restless, and too achy, to sit still any longer.

He got out of the car and decided to take a slow walk along Wilshire to kill some time, unlock his bruised-and-cramping muscles and burn off a little nervous energy. As soon as he hit the sidewalk, however, he felt exposed, as if he might be recognized at any moment.

He was so preoccupied with getting caught that he missed it on his first pass.

It was only when he was walking back toward the Chevy that he happened to glance off to his right and saw it parked down at the far end of an alley beside Kate's apartment block.

A white Cadillac.

The white Cadillac?

All at once Max went cold.

★ ★ ★

Before Kate could scream, Arena brought one rough palm up to cover her mouth and clamp her lips shut. His skin was hot and sweaty, and it stank of cigarettes and saffron, garlic and ground beef.

At last Tony finished unbuttoning her blouse and nodded approvingly when he parted it to reveal the lacy black bra beneath.

'Nice,' he said.

The room was dead silent.

He reached into his pocket and brought out a flick knife. He pressed a button on the side and the blade *snicked* out of the handle. She twitched, but Arena continued to hold her tight and still.

Very deliberately Tony slid the blade up between the bra cups. The tip did no more than graze her skin. Then he tugged the blade outward, the fine material parted and her breasts tumbled free.

Tony chuckled, low and throaty.

'Oh, that's sweet, princess.'

He refolded the knife and put it away, then reached for one of her nipples and pinched hard.

'That hurt?' he enquired.

Kate squirmed, her words muffled, indistinct.

'Easy, Tony,' said Arena, breaking his usual customary silence. He had a low, bubbly rumble of a voice. 'You're hurtin' the lady.'

Playing along with him, Tony shrugged his linebacker's shoulders. 'Guess I need more practice.'

He turned his attention to the other nipple, pinched that too, hard enough to send a jolt of pain through Kate and bring tears to her gray eyes. Again she struggled, tried to talk.

'Take your hand away, Ari,' said Tony. 'I can't hear what the lady's sayin'.'

Arena's hand left her face. Her jaw felt clammy, numb.

'I'll get you bastards for this,' she choked.

'Hey, listen,' said Tony, assuming an expression that was all innocence. 'It's nothin' personal, princess. I just wanna show you what can happen when Nick ain't around to protect you.'

'You guys're all heart,' said a voice at

110

the bedroom door.

Tony and Arena twisted around, expressions suddenly slack. They froze when they saw Max in the doorway, the .45 in his hand. Tony immediately raised his own hands, and pushing Kate aside, Arena followed suit.

'You again,' said Tony.

Max was trying hard to keep his rage in check, but it was difficult. The faintest tremor was already starting in his arms, and a bead of sweat was even now forming at his hairline.

Not now, he thought. And aloud he said: 'I told you I'd remember you, Tony.'

'Hey,' said Arena. 'We didn't hurt her bad.'

'And you're supposed to get credits for *that?*'

And that was it — the trigger that set him off.

He'd tried to control his anger and he'd done about as well as he could. But now, as it overwhelmed him and he blacked out and became someone else, he closed the distance fast and without warning and smashed Tony across the mouth with the barrel of the gun.

Tony grunted and fell sideways. Rather than wait to get the same treatment, Arena reached into his jacket, presumably for his own piece.

Kate turned and raked her nails across his ugly face, distracting him. Before he could stifle it, he gave a curious shriek and then Max was between him and Kate, and cracking the butt of the Colt against the fat man's temple.

Incredibly, Arena stayed on his feet. He lashed out and Max caught the full force of the blow against the side of his jaw and twisted away.

Arena went after him, not bothering with his gun now, knowing he didn't need a gun to finish this.

'*Max!*'

Kate's scream did something to stop him from going down and not getting up again. He straightened just as Arena grabbed him under the armpits and slammed him hard against the wall. Then the fat man started using his massive body to crush him.

Arena's head tipped to one side, his

thick, slack lips moving as he started whispering so that only Max could hear him.

'I'm gonna squash you like a bug,' he breathed, 'and you know what I'm gonna do when I hear your bones start crackin'? I'm gonna *come*.'

Still in pain from the night before, Max brought his free hand up and tried to hit Arena across the face, but the angle was all wrong and he couldn't get any force behind the blow.

Beyond Arena's shoulders he saw Tony wobble back to his feet, slap Kate and then make a grab for her. She dodged him, but only just, and kicked a stool into his path.

Closer to hand Arena, now too-too-clearly aroused, was whispering: 'I'm gonna enjoy this, bug-man, oh yeah I'm gonna enjoy this so *much* . . .'

'Enjoy *this* instead,' grated Max, and stuffing the barrel of the Colt into Arena's lard belly he pulled the trigger.

Muffled by all that fat, the gunshot was little more than firecracker snap of sound. Arena twitched, his pleasure-glazed eyes suddenly came back into focus and he said: 'You shouldn't have done that.'

Shocked, Max did the only thing he could, he shot him again, and this time Arena stumbled away from him, wobbling like Jell-O, and then seemed to corkscrew himself down to the carpet.

Trying to ignore the throbbing of his punished ribs, Max jumped over the body and threw himself at Tony before Tony could finally grab Kate.

He swung the flush-faced chauffeur around and hit him across the face with the Colt's barrel, opening a cut along one cheek. Tony reared away from him and started reaching for his own piece. Max closed on him, whacked him across the overlarge jaw with the butt of the automatic and again in the stomach. Tony went down on his knees, groping blindly for the overturned stool so that he could get his feet back under him.

Max was not about to allow that.

Again he smashed Tony on the back of the neck, just around the nape, then again, and again, and again, and Tony went down in increments, like a nail being hammered into a two-by-four.

At last he stopped moving and Max went to hit him again. It didn't matter that Tony wouldn't feel it. When he thought about what Tony and his buddy had been doing to Kate, how they'd been abusing her, he wanted to beat the pair of them to pulp.

But —

But . . .

Kate grabbed at him, and there was something in her touch that electrified him, shocked him back from that blackout world where he stopped being human and became instead something violent and remorseless.

He forced himself draw back from Tony, shivering and sweating all at once. He closed his eyes, forced himself to see —

— a winter scene, with snowflakes drifting slowly, silently to earth —

— a tropical island paradise with a resplendent magenta sunset dropping over a golden blue ocean —

— a scene from *A Day at the Races;* Groucho Marx taking someone's pulse and saying: 'Either he's dead or my watch has stopped.'

Kate stared at him, stunned by the change that had overtaken him and was even now leaving him again. She tried to speak but the words wouldn't come. She didn't think he'd have heard them, anyway, not right then.

After a little while she said: ' . . . Max?'

He nodded, looking like a man who'd almost puked himself inside-out. 'I'm okay,' he managed.

He looked around, froze when he saw Arena, covered in blood. 'Aw Christ, did I — ?'

She nodded. 'Don't worry about it. It was him or you.'

Besides, she thought, *you did the world a favor*.

Then something else occurred to her. 'Nicky's on his way over,' she said.

He felt the rage come surging back then. *Good. Let the bastard come. I'll be waiting for him, and we can finish this once and for all*.

But the idea sickened him even as he rejoiced in it. *Too much violence*, he

116

thought. *No more.* And again, Groucho Marx checked the patient's pulse and said: 'Either he's dead or my watch has stopped.'

'Get your things,' Max half-whispered.

'There's nothing left to get,' she told him. 'They trashed everything I had.'

He nodded, still shaky. 'All right. Let's get the hell out of here, *pronto*.'

13

By the time Nicky reached the condo they were long gone and Tony, barely conscious, was throwing up in the bathroom. Nicky let himself inside, went through to the bedroom and saw what was left of Arena on the floor, his big belly covered in blood.

He dropped to his knees beside the man and his face crumpled. *No, not Ari. Not Ari.*

'Tony!'

After a time Tony stumbled into the room. 'The bastard killed Ari,' he said.

With effort Nicky tore his eyes away from his dead friend. '*Who* killed him?'

'The bus-driver.'

Nicky's face went slack. 'That Max guy? Where the hell does he figure in this?' And then: 'Where is she? What the hell happened?'

Tony shook his head and flopped down on the edge of the ruined mattress. 'He got the drop on us,' he said. 'The guy's a freakin' psycho.'

'So she got away,' said Nicky. 'You let her get away?'

'You think I had any choice?'

'Hey, hey, you don't take that tone with me,' said Nicky, and he quickly pulled out a .38 and stuffed the barrel roughly against Tony's throbbing forehead. 'I wish he *had* killed you!' he raged. 'He would've saved *me* the trouble!'

Tony blanched, knowing that Nicky was more than capable of pulling the trigger, and had done so in the past, on people who were a lot closer to him and for reasons that were a lot less serious.

But then Nicky lowered the gun.

'You're lucky I'm a reasonable man,' he said softly. 'Now get a clean-up crew in here an' have them take Ari away. An' tell 'em I want him made beautiful again before we bury him.'

* * *

Still too shocked to know what to do for the best, Max drove them around for a while. *I killed a man*, he thought. *Whether he had it coming or not, I killed him.*

Maybe Aaron was wrong. Maybe I was capable of murdering Diana.

At last they found a quiet residential street and Max pulled to the curb and parked beneath some shade trees. They were quiet for a while, both remembering what had happened in Kate's apartment, Max having to imagine most of it because he had no conscious memory of it.

Finally Kate said: 'Max, I'm worried for you. About how you were today.'

He couldn't bring himself to look at her. 'I'm sorry. I didn't want you to see . . . what I can become.'

'You can't help that,' she said. 'But you *do* need to get help for it.'

He allowed himself a bitter smile. 'Just out of interest, what part of 'I'm on the run for murder' didn't you understand?'

'I know there's not a lot you can do while you're on the run,' she replied patiently. 'That's why we've got to sort this thing out once and for all. *One* of the reasons, anyway.'

'I wish I could, Kate, I really do. But the police have a pretty watertight case against me. And I can't even say for sure that I *didn't* kill Diana.'

'But there's that element of doubt, Max,' she said forcefully. 'It's an element we've got to explore, if only to lay it to rest once and for all.'

He sighed, knowing she was right. He owed it to Melanie — to Diana, too, if it meant bringing her real killer to justice.

He realized he should have solved the problem one way or the other a long time ago. Maybe Kate was one more reason to do it now. Trouble was, he was afraid of the answer, of finding out that he really *had* murdered Diana. He wasn't sure he could live with that. Hell, it was hard enough just to live with the idea that she'd been killed by someone else.

He suddenly heard himself saying: 'If I give myself up I've got no guarantees that the police will reopen the case.'

'Then we'll do it ourselves,' she said. 'And let's just hope you're right, Max — that you really *are* innocent.'

He finally looked at her. She looked

121

very serious, very determined, but still he wondered if she fully understood the enormity of what she was suggesting.

'Got any ideas about where we should start?' he asked.

She nodded. 'Yes,' she said. 'And we're going to start tonight.'

★ ★ ★

Dr Eric Danvil's medical practice operated from one of those old, stately, prestigious buildings that grace the flats near the post office in Beverly Hills.

A little after nine o'clock that night Kate climbed the steps to the building and rang the service bell. On the other side of the heavy glass security doors a gray-haired security guard looked up from the portable TV he'd been watching and frowned.

Kate gestured with one hand that he should come to the doors. He shook his head. She feigned desperation, bit her lower lip, walked a short, agitated circle and then allowed her shoulders to slump and mouthed: *Please . . . ?*

Grudgingly the guard got up and came across the lobby. He took a ring of keys from the belt that was almost lost beneath his paunch and unlocked the door.

'Go away,' he said. 'There's no one here. You'll have to come back tomorrow.'

'You don't understand,' she said wretchedly. 'My car's broken down. I've no idea what's wrong with the crazy thing. It was all I could do just to nurse it into your parking lot.'

He heard her out, then said: 'You'd better call Triple A.'

'I don't have Triple A,' she replied. 'I don't have *anything*. Look, could you at least just take a look at it for me? I can pay.'

'I don't want your money,' he said, but reconsidered when she took a fifty from her purse and handed it to him. 'Please,' she said again. 'I really don't need to be stranded out here right now.'

He chewed at the inside of his mouth for a moment, then said: 'All right. But I really shouldn't be doing this.'

'Oh, thank you!' she said, and started

back down the steps toward the parking lot.

The guard started to turn, intending to lock the door behind him, but she quickly started talking again to distract him.

'Could be I flooded it,' she said, 'or, well, you know, maybe it's a loose wire or something. Are you any good with cars?'

He shrugged. 'I get by.'

And figuring that if it was a loose wire it would only take a minute or so to fix it, he followed her down the steps to the adjoining parking lot.

★   ★   ★

Crouching in the shadows cast by a three-yard paper-recycling dumpster at the side of the building, Max heard Kate say: 'Cars — don't they just drive you nuts? Always breaking down, leaving you stranded in the middle of nowhere.'

'Lady,' the security guard reminded her as their shadows swept past, 'this ain't exactly *nowhere*. It's downtown Beverly Hills.'

When he judged that the voices were

far enough away, Max broke cover. He moved quickly and silently around to the front of the building, hurried up the steps and pushed at the doors.

He felt a sudden flare of excitement.

Yes!

Everything had hinged on Kate being able to get the guard outside and then hope he'd either forget to lock the doors behind him or decide it didn't really matter for the length of time he'd be gone.

So far, then, so good.

Ignoring the elevators, Max took the fire-stairs two at a time until he reached the second floor. He knew exactly where to find Danvil's office. Danvil had been his physician, too, until Aaron had taken over.

His heart was pounding now. If this went wrong, if the security guard came back before he'd accomplished what he was meant to do, then it was over even before it had started. Once he was detained by the police it was only a matter of time before they realized that the man who said his name was Max

Egan was really a wanted killer called Christopher Callan.

He stepped out onto the second floor. It was lit only by emergency lights at either end of the long corridor, leaving the middle portion in near-complete darkness.

He fumbled a pencil flashlight from his pocket, switched it on, cat-footed along the corridor until he reached the door marked *DR. E DANVIL*.

He looked at the lock for a moment before taking out a fake credit card he'd received in the mail a couple of months earlier. He slid the card into the crack between the door and the frame at a perpendicular angle and then leaned against the door. Guys in the movies did this all the time, and made it look easy. He knew from experience that it was far from that, but it *did* work, if you knew the right way to go about it.

Leaning a little harder on the door, he bent the card toward the left, until it was almost touching the handle. Slowly it slid in a little further.

Any moment now . . .

But the lock refused to cooperate. In an ideal world the door should have simply popped open. It didn't.

Which meant reverting to Plan B.

Keeping the card where it was, he started pulling and pushing the door so that it rocked back and forth in the frame, while at the same time trying to slide the card even deeper between the door and the lock. It wasn't anywhere near as impressive and it made a heck of a lot more noise, but this time it worked — with a click the door finally swung inward.

Max let himself in and shone the pencil flashlight around the room. He was in luck — Dr Danvil kept his patient records in two formats, stored on computer and protected by a password, and in old-fashioned paper files, kept in a gray-metal cabinet.

He went over to the cabinet and quickly checked the drawers. *A-H . . . J-N . . . O-Z.*

Using the credit card to force the lock, he opened the third drawer and leafed through the files until he found one marked, *Yasuda, Lynn.*

It had been Kate's idea to locate the so-called 'witness' who'd allegedly heard Max and Diana fighting and called the cops. If she had been lying on Danvil's behalf and they were somehow able to prove it, then the case against Max would fall apart, and at the very least give the police cause to question his guilt.

Now he opened the file, found what he wanted and hastily scribbled down an address and phone number. That done, he replaced the file and closed the drawer.

And that's when all hell broke loose.

14

Kate, now seated behind the wheel of the Chevy, turned the ignition.

The engine roared to life.

Kate's eyes widened in surprise and she smiled hugely. 'Can you believe that?' she asked the security guard. 'All this fussing around and it was nothing more than a loose . . . what did you call it?'

'Battery cable,' said the guard, slamming down the hood. 'Lady,' he added, 'if you're gonna drive a clunker like this, you ought to marry a mechan — '

He broke off as a Beverly Hills Police Department patrol car raced up, lights flashing, and squealed to an untidy, slanting halt in front of the building. Even as they watched, two cops leapt from the car with guns drawn.

'Holy shit!' muttered the security guard and started back across the parking lot, waving one oily hand to get their attention.

Kate watched him go, her face shadowing suddenly. *Oh Christ. I hope you're out of there, Max.*

*   *   *

Dr. Danvil's office faced onto the street, so Max heard the squeal of brakes as soon as the patrol car pulled up outside. All at once the room was filled with strobing red and blue light coming from the light bar bolted across the patrol car's roof.

Max allowed himself one passing moment of panic, then glanced around — and spotted the silent alarm set at ankle-level in the doorframe. He must've tripped it as soon as he stepped through the door.

The lights kept flashing.

Red lights . . .

. . . flashing . . .

And then he was back outside that alcohol-free bar in Fallujah, and there were bodies all around him, Marines who were unconscious or close to it.

He'd gone berserk, though he had no

memory of it. He'd taken them all on and they hadn't stood a chance against the rage that seethed within him.

Now a mixture of GIs and whores were looking at him, their expressions difficult to read. There came the sound of sirens, flashing red lights, and even as he whirled three MP's came charging into the bar and with a scream that was more animal than human he threw himself at them.

They clubbed him and he had no choice but to go down under the blows. But still he continued to scream: *I didn't run! I didn't run!*

As they cuffed him he heard voices above him.

What happened, man?

The captain kicked the shit out of those Marines, that's what happened.

What? Why?

They were messin' with his mind, man. Sayin' he ran out on his men.

But he didn't . . . did he?

Of course he didn't.

Chris — Max — was as certain of that as he could be.

But what about the other thing — what about Diana?

Suppose they hadn't said *he ran out on his men*. Suppose they said *he killed his wife*.

Could he be just as certain he hadn't done *that?*

* * *

When he was close enough the security guard called: 'What's goin' on?'

One of the cops countered with: 'You tell us. Call said you had a break-in. Silent alarm, second floor.'

The security guard blanched. 'Jesus — that'd be Dr. Danvil's office.'

* * *

Suddenly he came rushing back to the here and now. The lights were still flashing, exerting their hypnotic influence over him, but now he was able to fight it off. He moved across to the window, looked down, saw the police car and thought: *Shit!*

He quit the office, went back to the fire-stairs. But as soon as he started to descend he heard someone coming up from the ground floor — two men.

Cops.

He twisted around and went back into the darkened corridor. He thought briefly about the elevators, but they were probably switched off at night, and even if they weren't, where could they take him? To go up would serve no useful purpose. To go down would deliver him right into the hands of the security guard manning the lobby.

There was a window at the far end of the corridor. Maybe it led to a fire escape.

Behind him he heard the cops coming ever closer.

He went down to the window, looked out, swore. There were no stairs, no means of escape, just a drop of more than thirty feet, ending in —

Ending in the paper-recycling dumpster.

The paper-recycling dumpster that was filled with tied black bags.

Bags full of paper?

Shredded paper?

He wanted to think about this before he committed himself, but there was no time. Even as he backed away from the window the door to the fire stairs at the other end of the corridor crashed open and someone yelled: '*Police! Freeze!*'

Max looked back, saw the first cop standing at the other end of the corridor, adopting the classic Weaver stance preparatory to firing his gun.

Their eyes met.

Then Max thought: *Ah . . . hell!*

And ran straight at the window.

Just before he hit it he tucked his chin into his chest and brought his arms up over his head, and thought: *If this is security glass, I'm screwed*.

It wasn't.

It shattered as he went through it and shards of glass twisted and spun in all directions. Max himself hardly felt the cuts to his hands, he was too busy wondering what would happen if he missed the dumpster.

He went end over end and then slammed hard into all the bags. They sank under his weight but did what he'd hoped they'd do — cushioned his fall.

The air slammed out of his lungs and for one fleeting moment he thought he lost consciousness. Then he was pushing up, throwing himself over the edge of the dumpster, his legs crumpling beneath him.

Broken?

No — he got them under him again and started sprinting for the parking lot exit at the end of the alley.

Behind and above him the same cop yelled, *'Freeze!'* again, but again Max ignored him and just kept going.

Seconds later he heard an engine growl, tires squeal. The squad car came around the corner and its headlights lit up the alley.

Max's shadow surged out in front of him.

He kept running, leapt the chain that closed off the exit for the night, and then another car cut across his path and he ran right into it, cursed, bounced off.

It was a moment before he recognized the Chevy.

Kate yelled: '*Get in!*'

He wrenched open the door, threw himself inside, and she got them moving again even before he had the door shut. Their headlights swept the lot in front of them, found the entrance and Kate put her foot down and went for it.

The Chevy burst out onto the street, fishtailed wildly with smoke billowing up from under its shrieking tires. To their right the squad car reversed out of the alley, hoping to block them off. But quickly Kate twisted the wheel. Her car swerved, the right-side fender slamming against the patrol car. The impact crumpled the rear bumper against the back wheel and effectively took it out of action.

The cop behind the steering wheel pushed his door open and got out, gun in hand.

Max yelled: '*Go! Go!*'

She screamed back: '*I'm going!*'

She backed up the Chevy, away from the squad car, tugged the wheel hard to the left and they burned rubber as they raced off down the street.

Max drew a breath. He watched the needle touch eighty, then ninety. Danvil's building shrank in the rear-view mirror and suddenly the car felt more like a flying carpet.

Max held on grimly.

'You okay?' Kate asked without taking her eyes off the road ahead.

'I will be,' he replied. 'If we survive this.'

15

As soon as he got the call, Dr. Danvil drove straight to his office, where he was confronted by the two investigating officers.

Danvil was a tall, whip-lean man in his early fifties, with prematurely white, receding hair and a darker, neatly-clipped mustache. Under the eyes of the police he made a thorough inspection of his office suite and then said: 'Nothing appears to be missing.'

Officer Jackson, a short, blond man with faded blue eyes, said: 'It's possible we surprised him before he could steal anything.'

'I don't know what he'd have been after, anyway,' said Danvil. 'There's only a few dollars in petty cash, and we carry very few high-profile drugs.'

'Perhaps he's a patient of yours,' suggested Jackson's partner, Officer Torres. 'Or a former patient. Have you had any . . . difficulties . . . with any of your patients recently, doctor?'

'No.'

'Well, we got a pretty good look at the perp, and I made this sketch while it was still fresh in my mind. Does he look at all familiar, doctor?'

He passed his notebook across to Danvil, who studied it for a long moment.

'For some reason, we both think he looks very familiar,' prodded Jackson.

Danvil continued to look at the sketch, then handed it back and returned to the filing cabinets. He bent, slid open the third drawer and saw at once that the edge of one of the folders there was sticking out. He took the folder out, knowing whose name it would bear even before he saw it.

Sure enough, it read: *YASUDA, LYNN*.

He paled a little.

'I think I know who our thief is, officers,' he said quietly.

'You do? Who?'

'Christopher Callan,' he replied. 'What's more, I might also know where he's headed.'

★ ★ ★

Max held the scrap of paper to the passing streetlights and read the address and phone number again, then said: 'All right, I think we're safe enough now.'

Wordlessly Kate pulled over and switched off the engine, then finally allowed reaction to catch up with her.

'I could use a drink,' she said a little shakily. 'Where's a bottle of cheap bourbon when you need one?'

'Take it easy,' he said. 'It's over, now.'

He took out his cell and punched in the number he'd written down. The line rang a couple of times, and then a soft male voice said formally: 'Yes. Yasuda residence.'

'Mr. Yasuda?' said Max, suddenly dry-mouthed. 'I wonder if I could have a word with Lynn, please.'

The silence that followed his request was so long that Max thought they might have been disconnected. 'Mr. Yasuda?' he said again.

'We have nothing to say to reporters,' said the man at the other end of the line.

'Mr. Yasuda, I'm not a reporter. I just want a word with your daughter.'

'She is not here.'

'Then where is she?'

'We don't know,' the other man replied. 'She just . . . took off.'

'Hasn't she contacted you?'

No answer.

'Please, Mr. Yasuda. I can't tell you how important it is that I speak to Lynn.'

'I told you. We don't know where she is. Now please, leave us alone.'

This time the line did go dead.

'Damn!'

'What happened?' asked Kate.

'He didn't want to talk,' he said. 'My guess is that Danvil's already got to him.'

'So what do we do now?'

'I don't — '

He bit off as his cell buzzed. Since he rarely used the phone and never, ever gave out his number, he had no idea who it could be. After a moment he answered the call, said guardedly: 'Hello?'

The voice was young, female, pitched low as if afraid she might be overheard. 'You're looking for my sister, right?'

'Who is this?' he asked. 'How did you get this number?'

'Ever heard of last-call return?'

At that he relaxed a little. 'Okay. Who are you?'

'My name's Lisa. I'm Lynn's sister.'

'And you know where Lynn is?'

'I might.'

'How much? Is that the game?'

'Why not?' the girl countered. 'The other man didn't mind paying.'

'*What* other man?'

'The doctor,' she said. 'I don't know his name, only overheard him talking to my folks. But he gave them plenty.'

Max thought fast. 'I'll give you what I can, but it won't be anything like the payoff your folks got.'

'What are you offering?' she asked.

'All I've got,' he hedged, desperate and in no position to haggle. 'Two hundred dollars.'

'That's *it?*'

'Like I said, it's all I've got. Now, do we have a deal or not?'

'You know Stoner Avenue?' she asked.

'No.'

'It's just off Olympic.'

'I'll find it.'

'I'll be waiting for you on the corner,' she said. 'What are you driving?'

'A red Chevy.'

'You got thirty minutes to get there. If you're not there by then, forget it.'

'I'm on my way,' he said coldly and ended the call. Then, to Kate: 'If it's all the same to you — I'll drive from here on out.'

* * *

Lisa Yasuda was short and stocky, dressed in a short, tight black skirt, a red T-shirt and a gray shrug. She spotted them the minute they came around the corner and walked out to the curb to meet them.

Max pulled up beside her. 'What you got?' he asked.

She grinned at him. She had an oval face and greedy hazel eyes. 'The money first.'

He handed it over.

'I don't know the address,' said the girl, snatching the money out of Max's reach as he went to take it back. 'But you'll find it in the phone book,' the girl continued. 'Just look under Lynn *Yamoto*.'

He stared at her, trying to figure out if she could be trusted. 'This better be on the level,' he said. 'If it's not . . . I know where you live, remember.'

'It's on the level,' the girl replied easily.

They drove away.

Max was quiet for a while. Finally he said: 'I think it's about time we split up, Kate.'

She scowled at him. 'What?'

'The cops catch you with me, they'll hang an accomplice rap on you,' he said. 'You'll spend the next couple of years looking through bars, and I wouldn't want that.'

'Dammit, Max. You pick a hell of a time to get noble on me.'

'Not noble,' he said, 'just practical. After that stunt we just pulled back at Danvil's office, the heat'll really be on. You might not get a better chance to walk away from it.'

'Who says I want to walk away from it at all?' she countered. 'And even if I do, where do I go? Back to Nicky? No thanks — I don't think my nipples could take it.'

'You have other options.'

'Sure,' she agreed, and counted them off on her fingers. 'Run. Hide. Live out the rest of my days in Venezuela. Yippee.'

'Don't be a goddamn wise-ass,' he said. 'I don't think you realize just how serious this really is.'

'The hell I don't!' she snapped. 'Jesus, you must have really pegged me for an airhead.' She stared at his profile. 'Look, I appreciate your concern, Max. But I'm not ready to jump ship just yet. Okay?'

He made no immediate reply, but he was glad she had chosen to stay. After being so long alone, it felt good to have someone to share even this nightmare with.

Wanting to lay low for a while, they ended up at a small, rundown motel called the Ocean Breeze, in Culver City. There were no ocean breezes, only exhaust fumes from passing trucks. Only two cars occupied the parking lot when they drove in. Max switched off the engine and took out his cell again.

'You go register while I call Dr. Berg,' he told her. 'And for crissake don't use 'Smith'.'

Her smile chased away some of the strain in her face. 'Credit me with *some* imagination.'

As she headed for the office, he punched in Berg's number and let it ring. When Berg finally answered it he said simply: 'It's me.'

'Chris! What's going on?'

'I'm trying to sort this thing out once and for all.'

'By *yourself?*'

'No. I've got help. There's a girl who's come into my life. She's helping me.'

Berg let him have a long, disapproving silence. At last he said: 'I don't like it, Chris.'

'I'm sorry about that, Aaron, but that's the way it is. I tried to get rid of her but she wouldn't go, and frankly, I'm glad. She's the first good thing that's happened to me in a long time.'

Berg said grudgingly: 'Okay. I won't fight you on it. There isn't time.'

'Why? What's wrong?'

'The police came by earlier,' said Berg. 'Told me about the break-in, asked if there was anything in your case history that might indicate how you'd react next.' His frustration came out of him in a rush, then. 'Chris, what is it with you? Have you got a death wish, or are you just trying to incite a city-wide manhunt?'

'Neither. I needed to find Lynn Yasuda. This was the fastest way. And since *you* weren't getting anywhere — '

'I *was* getting somewhere!' Berg shot back. 'Any day now I expect to get Lynn's address.'

'My way was faster.'

'But mine wouldn't have tipped Danvil off to your next move,' Berg reminded him. 'You may have signed that girl's death-warrant, Chris.'

'How do you figure that?'

'If Danvil paid Yasuda to lie for him, then stashed her away somewhere, what do you think he's going to do now that he knows you're closing in on her? *Kill* her, that's what. Just like he did with Diana.'

'Then I'll just have to beat him to her.'

Berg's tone softened a little. 'Chris,' he

said gently, 'be careful. The cops say you're armed and dangerous. That means they won't be taking any chances. If they find you, they're gonna shoot to kill.'

'Well . . . let's just hope it doesn't come to that,' said Max.

But he had a lousy feeling that it might. It just *might*.

16

Berg stood there for a moment, then slowly replaced the receiver, so deep in thought that at first he didn't realize Elizabeth was watching him from the living room doorway.

At last he turned to her. A look passed between them, a knowing look that suddenly made him feel even more uneasy. What did she really know about him, he wondered, about *this*? How *much*?

Deciding to confront her, he said: 'Checking up on me again?'

The words slapped her. In the harsh overhead light she looked older than her years, joyless, lifeless. 'No. I just . . . I'm your wife, Aaron. I take an interest in you, in your work. If there's any trouble — '

'There isn't,' he told her snappishly. 'And there's no need for you to keep *spying* on me.'

'I'm doing no such thing!'

'Oh, come off it, Elizabeth. You still think I'm screwing around, don't you?'

She looked pained. 'Aaron, don't say things like that, *please*. You work hard and your job demands a lot from you. I *know* that. But I have needs too. I . . . I'm lonely. Having you home tonight . . . I don't think you fully understand just how rare that is, these days.'

He made no comment, because it was true and ridiculous to deny.

'Suppose we meet for lunch tomorrow?' she suggested, struggling to brighten.

'I can't,' he replied automatically. 'I've already arranged to meet . . . Dr. Monroe, at the VA.'

Her eyes dropped. 'Of course, darling.'

'Look, maybe the end of the week,' he said. 'Lunch, like you said.'

Without waiting for a reply, he started down the hallway toward his den.

'Aaron,' she said.

He turned, said, 'What?' and made it sound more like, 'What *now?*'

'I'm just looking for a little quality time, that's all.'

He nodded, and forced himself to

150

relent. 'I know. And I'm sorry. All right — lunch, tomorrow, at Pedro's.'

Her face lit up. 'Oh, Aaron,' she began.

He allowed her to come into his arms and he gave her an affectionate squeeze that he really didn't mean.

His entire career had been based on helping the emotionally needy, and it had made him a wealthy man. But as far as he was concerned Elizabeth went beyond needy, though he had never truly realized it until this moment. Elizabeth was downright pathetic, and all at once he was startled by just how much he despised her for it.

⋆ ⋆ ⋆

When all the packing material had been removed the following morning, Papa Crocetti got his first good look at the massive Kieninger longcase he'd bought at auction.

It was everything he'd hoped it would be.

In its elaborately crafted walnut case, with its signature curved base and walnut burl and inlays, it stood a little over six feet tall, two feet wide and more than a foot deep. It had two doors, six beveled crystal glasses, an elaborate brass moon dial with gold-plated fine grid, second indication and polished Arabic numerals.

It was so impressive that just for a moment Papa felt that he could have wept at the beauty of it. He bent forward to run his eyes appreciatively along the contoured lines of the lyre-shaped pendulum and matching grid and wondered just how much such a behemoth weighed.

'Where do you want it, Mr. Crocetti?' asked one of the men who'd just delivered it from the auction house.

The old man was so entranced by his new acquisition that he could barely tear his eyes away from its magnificent lines. 'Eh?'

'I said, where would you like us to set it up? We got to be careful, Mr. Crocetti. It's a beautiful piece, but it's kind of top heavy, liable to fall over real easy.'

Crocetti gestured to a spot beside the large fireplace. 'There.'

'Right you are.'

As the delivery men struggled to walk the clock into one of the few remaining gaps in Papa's wall-to-wall collection, there was a brisk rap at the open door and Tomasino glided in. 'I'm sorry to disturb you, Mr. Crocetti,' he said discreetly, 'but Mr. DiStefano's on the line.'

Papa, more interested in supervising the installation of his new Kieninger, waved him away. 'Tell him I'll call him back. I'm busy right now.'

'He said it's urgent, Mr. Crocetti. Something about the guy with Miss Winslow.'

Crocetti stared at him for a moment, torn between his desire to indulge his near-childlike excitement at the arrival of the clock and his need to find out about the man who had accompanied his Katarina to the house twenty-four hours earlier.

Eventually he nodded, went to his workbench, picked up the phone there and pressed a button. 'Speak quickly, old friend. I have no time to waste.'

He listened. Very quickly his frown slackened.

'Are you *sure* about this?' he asked. Then: 'Yes, yes . . . I understand. *Mille grazie.*'

Tomasino watched as he hung up and peered thoughtfully through the window at the sculpted grounds beyond. 'Bad news, Mr. Crocetti?' he asked carefully.

'The worst,' Papa replied, still in thought. Then, pulling himself together: 'Call Nicky. Tell him to get over here — now.'

* * *

Max's first job of the new day was to borrow a phone book from the motel office. He got a number and Winnetka address for the only *Yamoto* listed, then called the number but only got an answering service.

'Maybe she's screening her calls,' suggested Kate.

'Looks like we'll have to go visit her in person, then.'

Forty minutes later they got off the freeway and at the Roscoe Boulevard exit, turned right and drove toward Woodland

Hills. Another twenty minutes brought them to Winnetka, and the west-central San Fernando Valley home that Dr. Danvil had acquired for Lynn Yasuda.

The wide, busy boulevard ran in both directions, and keeping tabs on the street numbers, they turned right and found Lynn's house without much trouble.

It was a typical one-story, wood-frame ranch-style property, probably fifty years old, with a new fire-resistant shingle roof, Palos Verde stone front and a white corral fence around the big front yard. The grass was brown and withered from lack of watering and the yellow rose bushes on either side of the paved walkway were dying.

Max parked at the end of the street and together he and Kate walked back toward it. They waited for a car to drive past, then went up to the front door and Max rang the bell.

No one answered.

He rang the bell twice more.

Still no response.

Casually, he looked around. The street was empty. The husbands were at work, the kids at school, the well-heeled wives were out shopping or playing tennis.

'Come on,' he said.

'Where are we going?'

'If I can't speak to Lynn, maybe we can nose around and find some evidence.'

She balked. 'You're crazy! Evidence obtained like that's inadmissible.'

'All right. Let's just say that anything I can find will tell me whether or not what I think is true *is* true — that it was Danvil who killed Diana, and not me.'

They followed the path around the side of the house, through a gate, into a back yard with a blue swimming pool and finally came to the sliding glass patio door. Max cupped his hands to his eyes and peered through the glass. The living room beyond was light and spotless, everything in its place.

He looked down at the slider door. It was most probably locked by a latch. Or *was* it? On the chance that Lynn, like many other people with backyard pools, went in and out so often they got lazy and often forgot to lock the door, he tried it — and it slid open.

He should have known then that something was wrong.

He went in first, and having learned from the previous night's experience, checked around for any silent alarm sensors. He couldn't find any, but leaned up against the wall was a wooden dowel about three feet long.

Because sliders were so easy to jimmy, most people laid rods in the track to prevent the door from sliding open. But as with all seemingly perfect solutions, there was a catch: you had to remember to do it before you went out, and it was by no means unusual for house owners to forget.

Around them, the house was still and quiet. Leaving the living room, they quickly checked out the rest of the place. There were three bedrooms and two bathrooms, a large kitchen and a den.

And it was in the den that they found her.

'Ah Christ . . . '

She was dressed in a silver-colored silk robe, naked beneath, and she was sprawled half on her side, half on her belly, with her arms stretched out to either side of her.

She'd been shot once through the head, at very close range.

The bullet had made her skull appear as if it had collapsed in on itself.

Max swallowed. The carpet immediately beneath the entry wound was startlingly clean. At the back of the head, where the bullet had exited, however, the carpet was a muddy, bloody morass.

He spun around, grabbed Kate, turned her away from the sight and quickly led her from the room. Even the brief glimpse she'd got was enough to leave her pale, her lips bloodless, her eyes slightly glazed.

He felt like puking, felt his pulses hammering, knew he was heading for another blackout and fought it.

— a winter scene, with snowflakes drifting slowly, silently to earth —

— a tropical island paradise with a resplendent magenta sunset dropping over a golden blue ocean —

— a scene from *A Day at the Races*; Groucho Marx taking someone's pulse

158

and saying: 'Either he's dead or my watch has stopped.'

Now, as if from a long way off, he heard himself saying: 'We've got to get out of here.'

'But what about — ?'

'Lynn's beyond help,' he said, struggling to organize his thoughts. 'Did you touch anything?'

'What?'

'Fingerprints. Did you touch anything?'

'I don't think so.'

He took out a handkerchief and quickly wiped every surface he could remember touching. When they were back outside he gave the sliding door an extra wipe, did the same for the doorbell and then led her back around the house and down the street toward the car.

'Still want to stick with me?' he asked. 'I mean, Aaron was right, wasn't he?'

'Wh . . . what?'

'My friend, Dr. Berg. He said I might've signed Lynn's death-warrant. Looks like I did.'

They came to the Chevy, and all at once that raised another concern. 'We need to ditch this car,' he decided.

She nodded, her mind still in the house, the den, seeing the body of a once-attractive Asian girl of about twenty-three who'd never now get to see twenty-four.

'Kate?'

'What? Oh, yeah. Yeah. The car. And I need to go see Papa Crocetti.'

'All right,' he said, gathering his thoughts. 'Get a cab, go see the old man and try to settle this thing with Nicky once and for all. I'll go find someplace where I can trade the Chevy for a different set of wheels.'

She studied him closely. 'Will you be okay, Max?'

He nodded. 'Meet you back at the Ocean Breeze.'

17

Nicky watched his father wind the works of his new grandfather clock lovingly with a long brass key. The old man was enchanted by the mechanism — it was as close to poetry as he was ever likely to see.

Nicky said: 'You sayin' that jerk-off's really Christopher Callan? No way.'

'I'm afraid it's true,' said Papa without turning around. 'DiStefano's sources are immaculate.'

Finished with the winding, Papa took out a fob watch and carefully set the hands to the correct time, then set the pendulum in motion. If the craftsmanship of the piece was as poetry, then the ponderous tick-tock was a symphony to him.

'I can't believe it!' breathed Nicky. 'Kate's runnin' around with a fu — with a murderer?'

But it answered a lot of questions. The

guy had been a Green Beret. No wonder he'd been able to beat Tony half to death and take out Aristofani Arena without breaking a sweat.

Papa finally turned to face him. 'I too am disappointed,' he said. 'As you know, I had high hopes that you and Kate would . . . well . . . ' He paused briefly, then said: 'Have you ever heard a more melodious ticking?'

Nicky was momentarily sidetracked by the question. 'What? Oh, sure . . . sure. It's wonderful, Papa.' He was quiet for a moment, as his father shuffled around his workbench and eased himself up onto his stool. 'Did, ah . . . did Mr. DiStefano say where Kate and this Callan character are holed up?'

'No. It was the only piece of information he wasn't able to get.' But as an afterthought Papa added: 'Even his child doesn't know.'

Nicky frowned. 'Callan's got a *kid*?'

'A daughter called Melanie, apparently. She's a student at Sacred Heart.'

While Nicky considered that, the old man went on: 'I know it's hard, son, but you've got to put Kate out of your mind now. She no longer has a place at our table.'

Nicky sighed. 'Sure, Papa, sure. Who needs that kinda heat, right?'

Papa nodded. 'Now go. I'm expecting her here at noon. I don't want you here when she arrives, that would only be unpleasant and upsetting for both of you, and I want to keep this as quiet and civilized as possible.'

Nicky stared at him. Kate was coming *here*? Christ, that was perfect.

Keeping his expression neutral, Nicky nodded some more. 'Sure, Papa. Let's keep it . . . dignified.'

★　★　★

The high-class Mexican restaurant was elegant rather than trendy. Diners had to bring fat wallets to dine there.

Elizabeth Berg sat at the bar, realizing that there could no longer be any denying it. Aaron had stood her up. He'd known how important this lunch date was to her, and yet he had kept her waiting for forty minutes and finally texted — *texted*, not even bothered to call! — to say that his last appointment had over-run and he was having to work through lunch to make it up.

It might have been true, of course. There was always that chance. But at this late stage she was really past caring.

The truth was that Aaron would sooner be anywhere other than in her company. She didn't know why. She'd always tried to be the perfect wife. She looked after herself, ate sensibly, exercised regularly, was still a reasonably attractive woman for her age.

But Aaron didn't want *perfect*. He wanted something younger and nastier who would obey his every dark desire.

She finished her martini and ordered another. All at once she was sick and tired of Aaron and her thankless life with him. She didn't want to think about it anymore. But even as the thought occurred to her, an image flashed up on the wall-mounted TV playing silently behind the bar to remind her of what she'd lost, and to whom she'd lost it.

A cheerleader-blonde girl in her twenties.

Elizabeth quickly caught the bartender's eye with a gesture. 'Could you turn that up, please?' she asked.

'Certainly, ma'am.'

The barman reached for a remote control and sound faded up to join the images.

'. . . *friends, who say Carol Frost was under psychiatric care in the months leading to her suicide, are unable to identify the actress's lover, saying that Carol always refused to tell anyone his name. One thing everyone is positive about, however — Carol had been very dependent on this man, and was devastated when he recently broke off their relationship . . .* '

Elizabeth swayed dangerously on her stool.

No, no, no . . .

He'd gone too far this time. It was one thing for him to psychoanalyze these bimbos into bed, but another thing entirely to toy with their emotions until they felt they could no longer live without him.

She knew a moment of clarity then, when everything suddenly became so painfully clear to her — that Aaron was purely and simply a *user*. He told you what you wanted to here and then he used you until a younger, fresher, sexier model came along, and then you were dumped.

She saw, finally, that she too had been dumped, months ago — no, probably years ago. Only he had never really bothered to tell her, and she had been too stupid or naïve or in love to realize it.

Catching the barman's eye again, she ordered another refill.

★ ★ ★

It was a little after one when Max drove into the Ocean Breeze parking lot. Kate was just opening the door to their room. The first thing she heard was the clattering engine. When she turned and saw Max behind the wheel, and the car leaving a trail of smoke from its struggling exhaust, she decided she was having a particularly surreal nightmare.

166

She came forward to meet him, and as the old Toyota Civic pulled alongside remarked: 'Boy, you sure got the best of *that* deal.'

She wasn't telling him anything he didn't already know, but beggars couldn't be choosers right now. He got out, and had to make a number of attempts before the door would stay closed. 'Quit building up my confidence,' he replied. 'How'd it go with Papa?'

'Shitty,' she said bitterly.

'What happened?'

'He just said I was no longer welcome,' she told him. 'I said the least he could do was tell me why. He did.'

'And . . . ?'

'He knows about you,' she said, 'though God knows how. He said he didn't want the woman who bears his grandchildren to run with murderers.'

'That's nice, coming from someone who makes Don Corleone look more like Mother Teresa. What did you say to that?'

'I told him you weren't a murderer, and even if you were, I'd still rather be with you than that sadistic bastard he calls a son.'

'Ouch. I bet that went down well.'

'Let's just say I won't be holding my breath for a Christmas card this year.'

He sighed. 'I don't know about you,' he said, 'but I could *really* use a drink about now.'

'So go buy a bottle and we'll drown our sorrows before we decide what to do next. I think I saw a liquor store just down the street.'

'Good thinking, Batman,' he said. 'Won't be long.'

They split up. Max crossed the lot and Kate let herself back into their room.

A black Lincoln town car was parked across the street from the small row of stores that eked out a living along the nearby expressway. At Nicky's orders, its occupants — Tony and Bruno Corbucci, his broken right wrist now in a cast — had followed Kate all the way from Papa's house.

Max was just about to go into the store when Tony and Bruno intercepted him, Tony discreetly jamming his 9mm Smith

& Wesson none-too-gently into the small of his back.

'Get in the car, soldier,' he said, jerking his overlarge jaw in the direction of the Lincoln.

Max stiffened, but knew that resistance is futile when the enemy's holding all the aces. He allowed himself the luxury of cursing his lousy luck, then did as he was told.

When they were all in the car, it slid away from the curb.

'Where are we going?' Max asked tightly.

Tony grinned at him. He looked pale and his eyes were still shot through with blood following their last encounter.

'To see a man about a girl,' he replied.

18

They seemed to drive around aimlessly for a long time before they reached their destination, which turned out to be a disused service station. The Lincoln finally purred past a row of partly-demolished offices and garage bays until they swung right at the corner and pulled up in a garbage-strewn alleyway alongside a white Cadillac.

The Caddy was no surprise. Neither was Nicky.

Tony herded Max out of the Lincoln and into the back of the Caddy. Max slipped in beside Nicky, who was smirking at him.

Summoning a sense of confidence he in no way felt, Max said 'Love the new nose, Nicky. Must come in handy when you want to smell something that's around the corner.'

Ignoring that, Nicky said: 'Good of you to join me — Mr. Callan.'

'Mr. *Who?*'

'Gonna to tell me I got the wrong guy?' asked Nicky.

'Would it do me any good?'

'Not really.'

'So, what's your point, Nicky?'

'The point, *soldier*, is this. I could kill you right now and everybody would say I did the world a favor. You're public enemy number one, Callan. You're a goddamn *killer!*'

'So what's stopping you? Or do you plan to talk me to death?'

He thought Nicky was going to hit him. He looked like he wanted to. But when he finally moved, it was to take out a top-of-the-range cell phone. He punched in a number, waited a moment, then said: 'Carmine? Put her on.' He handed the phone to Max, grinned and said: 'One of your admirers.'

Max slowly took the phone, said cautiously: 'Hello?'

'*D-Daddy . . . ?*'

It was Melanie.

'*Daddy? I-is that you?*'

His whole world abruptly wrenched out

of true, Max stared at Nicky, but before he could do or say anything, Nicky took the phone back and ended the call.

Max felt his hands begin to shake. A bead of sweat trickled down into one eyebrow, then into the eye itself. Max didn't even flinch.

'You'd better kill me now, Nick,' he managed at last. 'Because if you don't, I'm gonna rip your throat out.'

'I don't think so,' said Nicky.

'What do you want?'

'You,' Nicky replied. 'Out of Kate's life. Forever.'

'What else?'

'That's it.'

Max frowned. 'You didn't need to snatch my daughter for that. All you had to do was turn me in.'

'I thought about that,' Nicky confessed. 'It was tempting. But then I realized that Kate might be the loyal type . . . would wait for you . . . no matter how long your sentence.' His smile died quite suddenly. 'This way,' he went on, his voice dropping lower with anticipation, 'when you dump her, she'll know that it's hopeless. An' I'll

172

have some fun making her crawl back to me.'

Max's mind was racing. But what the hell could he hope to do? As long as Nicky held Melanie, there was nothing.

'Take me to my daughter,' he said.

'Uh-uh. Not until I'm sure Kate knows it's over between you.'

Max reached up, wiped the sweat off his forehead. 'All right,' he said quietly. 'You win.'

'Did you ever think I wouldn't?' asked Nicky. And then, to Tony: 'Get this piece of crap out of here an' back to his motel.'

★ ★ ★

Kate was on him the minute he walked through the door. 'Dammit, where have you been?' she demanded. 'I was worried *sick* about you!'

'I told you,' he said tonelessly. 'I went to the liquor store.'

'And came back an hour later, empty-handed? Nice try, Max, but that was the first place I checked out. So how about the truth?'

He shrugged. 'I took a walk. Needed to straighten out my brains.'

She studied him uneasily. 'Why do I get the feeling I don't like the sound of this?'

'Kate, I — '

'Are you dumping me?' she asked.

'That's not the way I'd put it.'

'Who the hell cares how you'd put it?' she retorted. 'Why are you so determined to make history out of us?'

'I've had more time to think,' he said. 'And I don't . . . I don't want to lead you on any more.'

'Excuse me?' she asked. 'Lead me on? You trying to say that what we feel isn't mutual?'

'I guess I am,' he said, knowing he had to sell this but knowing equally well that his heart just wasn't in it. 'I'm sorry.'

'I don't believe you.'

'Why not?'

'Why not?' she repeated. 'Max, what's going on here? If you're trying to be noble again — '

'All right,' he snapped. 'I'll give it to you straight. I thought I had feelings for you, but I was wrong. I don't. All right?

And I don't want you around, either.'

Kate flushed with anger. She looked close to tears she would sooner die than shed. 'Kiss me and then tell me that,' she whispered.

He forced his tone to harden still further. 'I've got better things to do,' he said, and turned his back on her. 'I'm going out again. Don't be here when I get back.'

She watched numbly as he went out and slammed the door behind him.

* * *

As soon as Max left the room Kate collected her things together and followed him out. He didn't want her to be there when he got back. Okay — she wouldn't be.

But just as she rounded the corner she saw him further down the street, talking to someone in a Lincoln town car. She stopped dead, back-pedaled until she was hidden by the corner of the motel office. She knew that car well. And suddenly some of what had just transpired between them seemed to make sense. Nicky had gotten to Max somehow. That's why Max had dumped her!

The knowledge made her feel a little better about it, but only a little.

Max turned away from the Lincoln and started back toward the motel. Hurriedly she dodged into the reception and took a seat to one side of the greasy window. When she finally chanced a look around, she was just in time to see Max let himself back into their room.

She waited a little longer. A moment later he came out again, climbed into the decrepit Civic and drove away.

The minute he was out of sight she was up again and striding purposefully across the street and down toward the Lincoln. The big black town car was just pulling away from the curb, and she moved quickly to plant herself in its path.

When it slowed to a stop again she stamped around to the driver's-side door and rapped on the window. Tony let the window down and she said: 'Take me to Nick.'

Tony looked at her for a moment before saying: 'Get in.'

19

Max waited at the end of Hilgarde Street for probably the longest hour of his life before a taxi finally pulled up outside the old but immaculate two-story house where Melanie lived with Diana's sister Cora. He sat up straight as the passenger door opened and Melanie climbed out and ran up the steps to the front door.

Melanie — unhurt.

Max sagged with relief, felt fighting mad and close to tears at the same time. After a while he recovered himself, checked his immediate surroundings and then took out his .45 so he could check the clip.

That done, he tried to start the car. The engine turned over a few times before finally coughing to life.

Grimly, Max pulled away from the curb.

★　★　★

At Nick's penthouse condo, meanwhile, Nicky said: 'I don't know what you're talkin' about. I never told this Max guy to do anything. If he dumped you, he had his own reasons.'

Kate shook her head, her expression like murder. 'Bullshit, Nicky! I know you know who Max really is — your father clued me on that little eye-opener.' She tilted her head quizzically at him, as if he were a hitherto undiscovered bug that needed closer study. 'What did you do? Threaten to turn him in if he didn't unload me?'

He snorted. 'Dream on, baby. The guy dumped you. Deal with it.'

'The guy dumped me because he knew you'd turn him in if he didn't!'

'The cops'll find him soon enough, anyway,' he predicted.

'And when they do they'll be in for a surprise,' she replied. 'He's *innocent*, Nicky, he just can't prove it.'

'In a rat's ass he's innocent! My ol' man had him checked out six ways to Sunday. He's as guilty as sin.'

He expected an argument. She didn't

oblige him. Instead she treated him to another brazen stare that made his skin crawl. Finally she said: 'How much do you want me, Nicky?'

He grinned at her. 'Who says I want you at all?'

'Guess we have nothing to talk about, then,' she said.

She turned and was partway to the door when he stopped her with: 'Wait! What's on your mind?'

'A deal,' she said, turning back to him.

'What kinda deal?'

'Me, for as long as you want me.'

'And for that I do . . . what?'

'Help me prove Max is innocent.'

His laugh was a harsh, dismissive bark of sound. 'How the hell am I supposed to do that? Pay off the D.A.'s office?'

'Something much simpler,' she said. 'Something you specialize in, Nicky. Persuading uncooperative citizens to talk.'

His expression told her everything she needed to know. The proposition was finally starting to interest him. 'This particular citizen,' he said carefully. 'Who is it?'

'The real murderer,' she said softly.

★ ★ ★

Max went straight to Kate's apartment but she wasn't home — or if she was, she wasn't answering. Not that he could blame her. But what if she really *wasn't* home? Suppose Nicky was right, that having been dumped by Max, Kate had gone crawling back to him?

He remembered something then, something she'd said to him the first time they'd met: *I can't go back to my condo. It's only a block from Nicky's, and it's the first place he'll look.*

Nicky lived someplace close by, then.

He looked both ways. This was the Wilshire corridor, and luxury high-rise condos were the norm. Nicky could afford to live in any one of them. The question now was — which one?

But even as the question occurred to him, he realized he had a clue — Nicky's car. How many white Caddies could there be even in this affluent part of the city?

Find the car — find Nicky.

20

Dr. Eric Danvil regained consciousness slowly. At first he thought it was Sunday morning, and he was snuggled up safe and sound in the king-size bed in his Valencia home.

Then reality intruded, and it all came back to him in a sudden, stomach-churning rush.

Late afternoon:

He'd been leaving his office for the day, had climbed into his classic primrose Rolls-Royce convertible with the gold hubcaps and white leather interior, and was just pulling out of his parking space when a black Lincoln town car had backed out of the space opposite him.

The car had rammed into him and crushed his fender, and because it was an antique Rolls, Danvil had immediately seen red and jumped out to confront the other driver.

Except that the other driver was a big

man with a plaster cast on his right forearm and a held gun pointed at his naval.

Confusion, then:

Dear God — don't shoot! Here . . . you want my Rolex? Take it. My wallet, too. Just don't hurt me!

But this wasn't a mugging. Wordlessly the man struck him with the butt of his gun, a hard, swift jab that detonated an explosion inside his skull. He remembered falling but was unconscious even before he hit the tarmac.

And now —

He opened his eyes, realized at once that he had been tied and gagged and stripped down to his undershorts. Worse — he was hanging from some sort of hoist that was suspended from a rusty girder above, swaying like a bizarre human pendulum.

Panic engulfed him entirely then. He kicked his legs, shook his head, tried to jiggle from side to side and loosen his bonds, but they'd been tied too well.

He was breathing hard — as hard, that was, as the gag would allow. He felt hot and jittery and needed to pee.

As near as he could tell, he was in some kind of body-and-paint shop. It was early-evening, the doors were closed and the shop was lit only by a single light directly above his head.

Light puddled on the oily floor beneath him, broken only by his fuzzy, slowly-swaying shadow. The rest of the shop was dark and gloomy. He could just about make out the shapes of Mercedes and BMWs, all either damaged, partly-repaired or awaiting new paint-jobs.

He saw also that he was being watched by four people who were standing just beyond the light. Three men and . . . and a *woman?*

What do they want? What do they want?

One of the men stepped forward, his enormous, slope-shouldered frame encased in a well-cut black suit.

He was wearing goggles.

Goggles?

Then a second man came into the light. He too was wearing goggles, but Danvil recognized him immediately as the man who had knocked him unconscious in the parking lot.

This man, the one with the plaster cast on his right arm, was holding an acetylene torch, which he now lit.

The blue, needle-sharp flame popped to life.

Above the line of his gag, Danvil's eyes bulged with horror. He wanted to scream but the best he could manage was a series of terrified, muffled squeals.

'I'm gonna ask you some questions, doc,' said Tony. 'An' if I ain't happy with the answers, Bruno here's gonna turn you into a French fry.' He allowed Danvil to absorb that, then added amiably: 'Show the doc how it works, Bruno.'

Bruno adjusted the flame so that it was no more than a thin stiletto of heat, then applied it to a small, square sheet of metal that had been clamped to the edge of a nearby workbench specifically for this display. Sparks flew, and the metal began to darken before slowly, slowly turning amber.

The amber color brightened before Danvil's terrified gaze, became almost white, and then a hole developed and the flame hissed through to the other side.

'Get the picture, doc?' asked Tony.

Danvil wriggled and twisted like a fish on a hook. The sounds he made were impossible to translate, but the tone was clear enough — the poor bastard was shit-scared.

'Okay,' said Tony. 'Now, we'll keep this simple. You just nod for yes or shake your head for no. Got it? *Good* . . . Okay, here we go.'

His eyes found those of his prisoner.

'Did you beat Diana Callan to death?'

Abruptly Danvil stopped twisting and shook his head vigorously.

Tony tut-tutted. 'Wrong answer, doc,' he said with a tone of regret. 'Bruno — help the doc remember.'

Bruno advanced on the hanging doctor, raising the torch so that he could start with the soles of his feet. Danvil went crazy, thrashing around in mid-air, screaming his protests from behind the gag.

'Hold the sonofabitch still, will ya?' Bruno called to Tony.

Tony went around behind Danvil and held him still while Bruno ran the torch lovingly across Danvil's feet.

Danvil screamed.

Standing in the shadows, Kate had to turn away from the grisly sight. When she'd asked Nicky to extract a confession she hadn't dreamed it would be this . . . this . . . the word *barbaric* came to mind, but even that didn't really do the sickening spectacle justice.

'Stop it!' she pleaded. 'Please, Nicky! This is *wrong!*'

But Nicky was enjoying the show. Sometimes he never felt more alive than at times like this. 'Shut up!' he said without looking at her. 'You asked for the truth. I'm gettin' it.'

And getting a hard-on at the same time, she thought.

★ ★ ★

At one of the smudged windows outside the repair shop, Max was torn between revulsion at what he was witnessing and his need to hear Danvil confess.

He'd spent a fruitless couple of hours cruising back and forth within a one-block area before finally striking it lucky.

He'd spotted the white Caddy just as it pulled out of a subterranean garage beneath the condo where Nicky must have his apartment. After that it had been a matter of tailing the car as discreetly as possible — no easy thing when the car you were driving was a coughing, spluttering Toyota Civic that attracted attention for all the wrong reasons.

The Caddy had turned left on Beverly Glen and headed south to Olympic. The traffic was heavy and Max had had trouble keeping the Caddy in sight.

Finally the limo turned south onto a side street lined with industrial buildings, warehouses and auto body-shops. Forced to keep well back now, he'd eventually lost the car and had to cruise around again until he finally spotted it parked outside the repair shop, beside the equally-familiar black Lincoln.

He'd parked on the street and walked back. And now here he was, watching his wife's murderer being tortured and wanting to stop it because he actually felt sorry for the guy.

He forced himself to wait, to watch, to listen.

★ ★ ★

The torture finally over, at least temporarily, Tony came back around and stared straight up into Danvil's twisted, sweat-run face. 'How about it, doc? Ready to change your mind yet?'

All Danvil could do was use his pain-glazed eyes to plead his case.

But that cut no ice with Tony.

'Again, Bruno,' he said.

Again Danvil's gurgling, muffled screams filled the workshop.

'Is that a yes, doc?' Tony asked expectantly. He had to shout to be heard above the roar of the blowtorch. 'Did you kill Diana Callan?'

Near to fainting, Danvil stubbornly shook his head.

Tony turned and looked at Nicky. 'Want us to continue?' he asked.

Nicky looked at Kate, enjoying the revulsion he saw in her expression. 'Well?' he asked. 'Your call, baby.'

Outside, Max turned away from the window, the world, as he knew it, suddenly dropping out from under him.

Could Aaron have been wrong about Danvil? Surely the guy would confess to just about anything to stop that kind of pain . . . *wouldn't* he?

And yet Danvil had shook his head firmly.

So if he really *hadn't* done it, who had?

You did, he thought.

No, he couldn't have! He wouldn't have done it, no matter how bad the marriage had gone. And yet it *had* gone wrong. *Badly* wrong.

But wrong enough to commit —

★   ★   ★

As Bruno and Tony stood beside the twitching Danvil, Nicky said: 'Well? Satisfied his tellin' the truth, or what?'

Kate swallowed. She wanted to be sick, not only because of what she'd just witnessed, what she had asked Nicky to do to this poor man, but because his refusal to confess could only mean one thing.

That he really *was* innocent.

She was just about to nod when Nicky's cell phone rang. He snatched it out, checked the caller ID, then said: '*Ciao*, Tomasino. What's up?'

Kate watched the blood drain from his face.

He said: 'When?' And then: 'Is he . . . ?'

Nicky actually rocked back on his heels.

'I'll be right there,' he said, and ended the call.

Tony came back out of the circle of light and tugged his goggles off. 'What is it, Nick?'

'It's Papa,' Nicky said vaguely. 'There's been an accident. He's dead.'

'*What?* The old man *dead?*'

Tony was immediately at Nicky's side, reaching out to steady him, but Nicky swatted him away. 'Get offa me!' he barked.

A moment longer he stood there, staring into space, struggling to accept

190

what had happened. At length he collected himself enough to say: 'Cut that creep down and then come to the house.'

He grabbed Kate by the arm and dragged her out of the repair shop with him.

21

Max waited until they'd gone, then let himself into the repair shop. As much as he wanted to go after Kate and take her away from Nicky, he felt that she would be safe enough for the moment. Right now Nicky had other things to concern him.

He switched the light on and saw Danvil curled into a ball in the middle of the cold, oily floor, where Tony and Bruno had dumped him.

Danvil, untied now, and with the gag removed, was shivering and sobbing.

Max looked around, spotted the doctor's clothes in a pile and went to get them. He took them back to Danvil and set them down beside him.

Danvil, suddenly realizing that he was no longer alone, twitched and curled himself even tighter. 'No . . . no . . . *please* . . . '

'It's all right,' Max said in a soft voice choked with guilt. 'It's all right. They've gone. I'm going to call 911 and they'll be here before you know it.'

He felt sick with the knowledge that he'd been living a lie all these months, kidding himself that someone else had killed Diana, when all along —

But more than that, he felt sick for the way this man, this *innocent* man, had been forced to suffer.

He made a quick inspection of Danvil. The doctor looked dreadful, his bare feet black and blistered. Max sagged and thought: *What have I done? What did I ever do to cause so much misery and suffering to just about everyone around me?*

Danvil stopped shivering, dared to look back at him from across one bare shoulder.

They looked at each other for a taut, silent moment. Then, recognizing Max, Danvil grabbed him by the shirtfront. His eyes were dark shadows, but the fury in them was so palpable that you didn't have to see it; you could *feel* it.

'Hang on,' Max croaked. 'I'll get help — '

Danvil spat in his face, followed it with: '*Murderer!*'

Max flinched back from him, knowing it was true, that it had *always* been true, that no amount of denial was ever going to change it.

He backed away from Danvil, took out his cell and forced his trembling fingers to punch in 911. Danvil started sobbing again as he requested an ambulance.

Max got out fast, before it arrived.

★   ★   ★

He climbed into the Civic and drove across town to the house on Hilgarde where Melanie lived with her Aunt Cora. He parked outside and sat there for a long time.

He felt numb, and yet relieved at the same time. After all these months, he finally knew the truth. No more doubt. All he could do now was accept the consequences, as he should have done months before.

He got out of the car, went up the steps to the front door and rang the bell. A few

194

moments passed and then it was answered by a small, rounded woman in her middle-forties. The polite expectancy on her pleasant face turned to shock when she saw Max standing there, and she instantly tried to close the door again.

He'd been expecting that, of course, and quickly stopped her. 'Cora,' he said softly, 'wait.'

'Get away from here, Chris, or I'll call the police!' she said.

'You don't have to,' he said. 'I'm turning myself in.'

Again she registered surprise. 'Then what are you doing here?' she managed at last.

'I want to say goodbye,' he said, trying to keep his voice level. 'To Melanie.'

'You can't,' Cora said immediately. 'She's asleep.'

'Cora, I'm coming in.'

She looked into his eyes, saw how tired he was, how used-up, and surprising no one more than herself, she took pity on him. He went inside, nodded his thanks, and without another word went softly up the stairs until he reached Melanie's bedroom.

He opened the door. Light from the hallway fell inside, showing him a typical ten year-old girl's bedroom. And there, in the bed, her light brown hair fanned out across the pillow, the girl that was his whole world lay sleeping.

He crossed the room silently, stood there for a while just watching her, storing up his memories of her, the smell of the room, the soft sound of her breathing, then bent and gently kissed her forehead.

She stirred, blinked, focused on him.

'Daddy?' she said sleepily. And then, sitting up quickly: '*Daddy!* Some men took me away from school this afternoon — '

'I know all about that, kitten, and I'm sorry. Did they hurt you?'

'No. They just said I had to wait for someone to call, and sit still, and nothing would happen to me.'

'Well, forget them,' he said. 'They'll never bother you again, kitten, I promise.'

She nodded, trusting him completely. 'What're you doing here, Daddy?'

'I came to tell you something,' he said, dropping to one knee so that they could speak face to face. 'I'm going to do what you suggested, kitten. I'm turning myself in.'

Her eyes went large. 'You *are?*'

'This way, like you said, we'll be able to see each other — when you come for visits.'

For the first time the girl thought about what it was really going to be like for her father. 'Prison's awful nasty,' she said. 'Will you be all right?'

He had to struggle to keep his voice even, and was glad that the light was behind him, so that his face was in darkness. 'I'll be fine, sweetheart,' he promised gently. 'But I have to go now. You be a good girl, and do whatever Aunt Cora tells you, okay?'

'I will, daddy,' she said.

And then the tears came.

He'd been dreading it, and as she started crying and reached her arms up around his neck, he had to dig deep to hold his own tears at bay.

'I'm going to miss you so *much* . . . '

Melanie whispered.

'You too, Mellie,' he managed.

He kissed the top of her head, her forehead, her face . . . then finally pulled away and left the room.

Melanie stared after him, lower lip trembling, tears rolling down her cheeks.

*   *   *

At the door he looked at Cora and said softly: 'Thanks.'

Cora looked back at him strangely. Regardless of what she'd always told Melanie, she herself had never doubted that Max — *Chris*, as she had always known him — had killed her sister.

But now there was something other than hostility in her eyes; for the first time she seemed to doubt the very thing she had until now always believed so implicitly.

'You don't have to worry,' she said after a while. 'She'll be all right.'

'I've always known that, Cora,' he said simply.

He was halfway down the steps to the

sidewalk when she called his real name. He stopped and turned back. There were tears in her eyes.

'Thank you,' she said.

He looked puzzled. 'What for?'

'For doing the right thing at last,' she said. 'Diana will rest easier now. We all will.'

He continued on down to the waiting Civic and climbed inside. Behind him, Cora closed the door softly. He slowly leaned forward until his forehead was resting on the steering wheel.

When he'd finally gathered himself, he cleared his throat and took out his cell phone. He keyed in a number and listened to it ring.

A moment passed and then a voice at the other end said: 'Berg.'

'Hi, Aaron. Can you talk?'

'Sure. I'm down here at Sawtelle right now, catching up on patient notes, so I've more or less got the place to myself. What's happening?'

'I'm turning myself in,' said Max.

'You're *what?* Now hold on, Max. Don't do anything hasty till we can talk — '

'There's nothing to talk *about*, Aaron. I just wanted to let you know. As soon as I hang up, I'm going to the cemetery for a few minutes, and then I'm turning myself in.'

He didn't need to explain about the cemetery — Berg knew how much time he usually spent at the VA National Cemetery in Sepulveda. It always gave him a rare sense of peace to be among his comrades.

'B-but why the sudden about-face?' Berg asked.

'Simple,' Max replied tiredly. 'I think I'm guilty.'

'What about Danvil?'

'He's in the clear, Aaron. I know that now.' He reached up, used the fingers of his free hand to rub at the flesh between his eyes. 'If you come down to the police station in about half an hour, I'll give you all the details.'

It wasn't open to debate; his mind was made up. So he ended the call and turned the key in the ignition.

The Civic refused to start.

He groaned. 'Ah, not now . . . '

He tried again, but still the engine refused to turn over.

Someone's trying to tell you something, he thought.

He punched the steering-wheel, got out and slammed the door behind him. It didn't catch, just swung open again.

He looked back at the house, thought he saw a curtain twitch at one of the upstairs windows — not Melanie's, thank Christ.

He opened the hood, checked the battery cables, slammed the hood shut again and got back behind the wheel. Again he tried the engine. It turned sluggishly, but still it died on him.

The perfect end to the perfect day, he thought acidly.

It took another ten minutes of tinkering with the battery cables before the Civic finally started. Even then he had to coax the old car all the way to Sepulveda.

He'd said his goodbyes to Melanie. Now he'd say his goodbyes to all the men who'd died while he, for some reason he knew he would never understand, was spared. The only regret he had left was that he wouldn't get to say goodbye to Kate.

As he approached the cemetery, however, he saw about four or five police cars parked haphazardly around the entrance with their light-bars flashing, and felt an immediate stab of alarm.

He slowed a little and leaned forward across the wheel. In the deeper darkness of the cemetery itself, thin, dancing bars of yellow light swept up, down, left, right.

Flashlight beams.

The police were searching for someone.

Him?

The familiar uneasiness resurfacing in him, Max drove right past without stopping.

And something extremely unpleasant suddenly occurred to him.

As soon as I hang up, he'd told Aaron, *I'm going to the cemetery for a few minutes, and then I'm turning myself in.*

Aaron was the only one who knew where he was going.

Aaron . . .

And what was it that Lisa Yasuda had said to him, last night on Stoner Avenue? *The doctor. I don't know his name, only ever overheard him talking to my folks.*

202

But he gave them plenty.

The doctor.

The *doctor* . . .

Reaching a decision, Max turned into a side-street and pulled over, then snatched out his cell and punched in the Yasuda's number.

When Lisa's father answered he said: 'Don't hang up.'

There was a moment of silence. Then: 'What is it you want? My Lynn is dead. She was murdered.'

'I know, and I'm sorry for your loss,' he replied. 'In a way, that's why I'm calling.' He hesitated before committing himself, then said: 'I know who killed her, Mr. Yasuda. It was Dr. Berg.'

There was no immediate response, but then: 'Impossible! He's the one who — '

' — paid you to keep quiet?' Max finished.

Another pause, longer this time. At the end of it Yasuda said in a small voice: 'Yes.'

Max nodded, starting to feel sick all over again. 'Thanks,' he said. 'That's all I needed to know.'

22

Berg was sitting at his desk, but turned around with his back to the door so that he could stare out through the large window at the sleeping city beyond. He was also doing something relatively unusual for a psychiatrist — he was chewing his nails.

When he heard the door click softly behind him, he knew that it was all over. Something had happened, he knew it. Perhaps he'd said or done something to give himself away; whichever, Max had finally put everything together.

He stiffened but didn't turn when he saw Max's reflection in the glass before him.

'It's over, Aaron,' Max said quietly.

Slowly Berg spun himself around until they were facing each other. His face looked pasty, sick, but still he tried a denial. '*Over?* What do you — ?'

It was the denial that angered Max

most of all, though he couldn't really say why. Suddenly it all boiled to the surface: Berg's treachery, Berg's betrayal, and he came around the desk and grabbed Berg's shirtfront and yanked him up out of the chair until their faces were just inches apart.

'I just want to know why, that's all,' he rasped.

Cringing under Max's glare, Berg said: 'It . . . it's complicated.'

'Then I'll uncomplicated it,' grated Max. 'Why did you kill Diana?'

'She was blackmailing me.'

'About what?'

Berg squirmed. 'Listen . . . Chris . . . can't we talk about this another — '

'*About what?*'

Berg refused to meet his eyes, looked away and muttered something Max didn't quite catch.

'What was that?'

'About raping her during our session,' Berg repeated in a whisper.

Max pushed him away and Berg fell back into his chair, his tie twisted all out of shape.

'Diana was a patient of yours? When?'

'The last year of your marriage,' said Berg. 'She came to me because she felt you didn't love her any more . . . felt so rejected by you that she was considering suicide.'

'So you felt obliged to prove that someone still desired her?'

'Chris, I *swear*, she wanted it as much as I did. More, in fact.'

'Then where does rape fit into it?'

Berg made a meaningless gesture with one hand. 'In her emotional state, she attached more significance to . . . what happened . . . than I did. Insisted we get married. When I refused, she became hysterical, threatened to go public and press charges, claim that I'd raped her during therapy.'

'And that justified killing her?' asked Max. 'Wasn't that just a bit *extreme*, Aaron?'

'You don't understand,' Berg said quickly. 'My whole practice is built on patient-doctor trust. Even if Diana's charges hadn't stuck, it would have seriously undermined my credibility. I couldn't have that.'

'So you beat her to death and let me take the rap for it.'

'That wasn't the intention, I swear it. I never meant for you to take the blame. It just . . . worked out that way.'

'Kinda convenient, though, wouldn't you say?'

'Chris, I wanted to come forward when you were arrested,' Berg said miserably. 'God, you don't know how many times. But I just couldn't make myself. But I *did* help you escape. That's worth something, isn't it?'

'I always thought so — till now.'

Berg frowned. 'What do you mean?'

'It's taken me a while,' said Max, 'but I've finally figured out why you did help me — the real reason, I mean. In prison I'd always be a threat hanging over you — the possibility of new evidence coming to light, a retrial, clues leading back to you. Who knows what might have happened.'

'Chris, that's crazy talk.'

'But out on the street,' Max continued, 'a convicted murderer on the run, armed and dangerous, with a history of violent blackouts . . . hey, chances are that the cops would gun me down the minute they found me and end all your worries.'

'Chris, that isn't the way it was, I swear. You're all mixed up — '

But Max was relentless now. 'You even encouraged me to go after an innocent man — Danvil. What was he, a professional rival?'

No answer.

'Aaron?'

'Something like that,' murmured Berg.

'And then, when I got too close to her, you killed Lynn Yasuda,' said Max. 'The girl you paid to 'witness' my killing Diana. What was she, another one of your conquests? Willing to do whatever it took for her dashing doctor' He shook his head, disgusted. 'Jesus Christ, Aaron, I've got to hand it to you — you left no rock unturned.'

Silence poured into the room.

'So . . . what happens now?' Berg asked quietly.

'What do you think happens?'

Trapped now, Berg attempted to

summon up some confidence. 'I think you don't have one shred of hard evidence against me,' he said. 'I paid the Yasudas in cash, Lynn included. It'll be your word against mine. And I think we both know whose word the law will believe.'

Max grinned coldly. 'That's something we'll just have to find out, isn't it?'

Berg's unease made a return appearance. 'You're still planning to turn yourself in, then?'

'*Count* on it.'

Max went back around the desk, not sure how he felt now that he had the truth. Relieved? Disappointed?

Then Berg said: 'I don't think so, Chris.'

There was something in his tone that froze Max in his tracks.

'Now, turn around,' Berg continued. 'Slow. No sudden moves.'

Max did as he was told, cursing himself when he saw that Berg had taken a small, nickel-plated Smith & Wesson .45 ACP Chief's Special from his waistband and had it pointed rock-steady at Max's stomach.

He realized that he was in all likelihood looking at the same gun that had killed Lynn Yasuda.

'This is perfect,' Berg said, excitement creeping into his tone. 'You came in here, threatened me, and I had no choice but to shoot you.' His smile was more of an anticipatory twitch. 'After all, who knows more about how dangerous you are than your own doctor? Now, get back over here, by the desk.'

Max fixed him with a hard stare. 'Don't point that gun at me, Aaron.'

But Berg was no longer listening to him. Quickly he messed up his hair, knocked his chair over, swept the papers on his desk to the floor. 'There, that should do it,' he muttered. And then, with what seemed like genuine regret, he said: 'Sorry, Chris.'

Max looked him straight in the eye.

Within the confines of the room, the gunshot sounded twice as loud as normal.

But it was Berg who suddenly staggered and grabbed at his belly, Berg who stared down in disbelief as blood started weeping from the wound in his stomach and the searing stab of hot lead jagged through him.

He looked up again, his mouth open. He looked into Max's face, saw his own shock mirrored there, then turned a fraction, stumbled — and froze when he saw Elizabeth standing in the doorway.

Elizabeth, holding her own small gun waist-high, tucked in tight to her hip, smoke wisping lazily from its barrel.

Then his eyelids fluttered and the eyes themselves rolled up into his head and he fell to the carpet, dead.

Max turned slowly, carefully, and stared at her, not sure what was going to come next. But Elizabeth seemed hardly aware of his presence.

'Now he'll never be able to hurt anyone ever again,' she whispered. She blinked rapidly a few times, until her eyes found him at last. 'Not even you,' she added.

'Elizabeth,' he said, 'you better call your lawyer.'

'I will,' she promised. 'Right after I call the police and tell them everything I just heard Aaron tell *you*.'

They both became aware of running

feet — security staff alerted to the gun-shot. 'Get out of here, Chris,' she said.

Unable to find any other words, he could only nod.

23

Nicky stood in Papa's cluttered work-shop, staring down at the enormous Kieninger grandfather clock, which lay on its side, one brass-tipped edge stained dark with his father's blood.

Beside him, Tomasino said: 'We kept tellin' him it was gonna fall over, Nicky. We even offered to nail some boards around the base, you know, to help support it, but your papa wouldn't hear of it. He said you don't add paint to a van Gogh.'

Nicky was aware that he was speaking, but his mind was elsewhere. 'You loved that old clock, didn't you, Papa,' he whispered.

Tomasino fell silent and threw an uneasy look across the room to Kate, who was balancing on the edge of the couch, hugging her knees.

'Go, now, Tomasino,' Nicky said suddenly. 'Go on, get out of here. I want to be alone.'

Tomasino raised his eyebrows at Kate, as if to say: *You comin'*?

But it was as if Nicky read his mind. 'Not her,' he said quickly. 'Just you, Tomasino. Get out of here. I need to grieve. We need to grieve.'

Kate met Tomasino's eyes and nodded slowly.

I'll be okay.

I hope.

At first Nicky had raged against whatever cruel fate had decided to take his father away from him. He'd kicked everyone out, saying he wanted to be alone, but not *completely* alone.

The truth was that the reality of his situation had finally struck home. He was an obnoxious little prick hated by just about everyone with whom he'd ever come into contact. He had no real power of his own. His only claim had ever been that he was Papa Crocetti's son. That had bought him a measure of grudging respect and immunity.

But now Papa Crocetti was dead. That safety net was gone. And Nicky knew that once the word got out, all the enemies he'd ever made would be standing in line to get back at him.

Much as he tried not to acknowledge the fact, Nicky was now living on borrowed time.

'Truth is,' he said suddenly, still speaking mostly to himself, 'he loved every clock in this house. They . . . they were like children to him, and that's the way he treated them.'

Kate watched as he slowly continued to lose his mind.

He finally flopped down on Papa's stool and slowly pulled out his Browning 9x9mm Hi-Power automatic. His eyes wandered to Kate, but all he saw was the couch she was sitting on.

'Remember all the naps you took here, Papa?' he said, deftly working the weapon's slide. 'Every day for twenty years, at two o'clock exactly. Not a second before, not a second after. Right, Papa?'

Kate felt her muscles cramping, but was reluctant to move. If she moved now she might jar Nicky out of whatever mental padded-cell he was in. And if she did that and he didn't want to come back yet, he might turn mean.

At last Nicky looked up and around, his eyes restless, lingering in no one place any longer than they had to. Without warning he brought the gun up and fired it at one of the room's overabundance of clocks. The clock face exploded with a shatter of glass and a hollow thrum of coiled springs.

'Even when we lived in New York,' Nicky continued as if nothing had happened, 'Papa always took his naps. Right, Papa?'

Now Nicky stood up, wandered across to one of the older clocks in the collection. He studied the piece for a while, then said: 'Remember when you bought this one, Papa? I do. I was only eleven, an' — '

Behind him the door opened, and Nicky frowned. The house was empty. He was in mourning and wasn't to be disturbed.

He turned and stared at the man he knew as Christopher Callan, frowning because he shouldn't be here, no one should. Just him, his memories . . . and Kate.

Kate stared at Max, her mouth dropping open.

Ignoring her, not daring to take his eyes off Nicky, Max said: 'Mind if I join the wake?'

Nicky cocked his head at him. 'Ain't you got no *respect*, Callan?' he asked. 'A man *died* here today! My Papa! I'm grievin', you sonofabitch!'

'Papa's in hell, Nicky,' said Max, slowly coming deeper into the room. 'And you know what? I'm gonna send you to keep him company.'

'Max . . . ' Kate hissed.

'Don't mess with me, Callan,' said Nicky. 'Not unless you want your daughter's schoolin' cut short.'

That did it. Mention of Melanie was all it took to make Max snap. All at once he came across the floor faster, closing the distance between them, and Nicky jabbed the Hi-Power at him and fired.

Max went low, dove forward and took Nicky around the legs. Nicky went backwards and down, and Max, now on all fours, started climbing up him before he could use the Hi-Power again.

Nicky brought the weapon up and Max batted it aside. Nicky's finger tightened on the trigger and somewhere behind Max another clock exploded.

Max — or whatever creature he became during these blackouts — punched Nicky in the face and while he was gurgling pulled the gun from his hand and tossed it aside. Then he dragged Nicky back to his feet and slammed him hard in the side of the head.

Nicky went sideways, crashed into an antique longcase from Austria. He hit it so hard that the wood splintered, the glass front cracked. Nicky bent, recklessly shoved his hands through the broken glass and tore the heavy brass pendulum from the case and then threw himself back at Max.

He tried to use the pendulum like a club. Max backed away from him, narrowly avoiding each vicious swipe, sidestepped one especially wild charge, then grabbed Nicky by the back of his head and the small of his back and ran him forward, mercilessly, straight into a *Comtoise* that tipped and shuddered under the impact.

Nicky stumbled and wheeled drunkenly, his face a mask of blood, his nose even more misshapen than it had been before. Max tore the pendulum from his grasp, hurled it away, threw himself back at Nicky.

Nicky, roaring now, let him come and got in a lucky punch. Winded, Max could only take the kick with which Nicky followed it, and while he was still hurting Nicky punched him again, a clubbing blow to the top of the head. He fell back, another longcase splintered and shattered beneath his weight.

Nicky jabbed. Max dodged and Nicky's fist smashed glass and his fingers snagged on the fine, spindly hands of the *Moonroller*. Max grabbed him by the shoulders, whirled him around, hit him again, again, and Nicky went back, glass crunching underfoot, stumbling on the ruined shards of what had once been Papa's beloved collection.

He went down then, and Max went right down on top of him, hands numb but still balled into fists. He sat on Nicky and punched and punched and went on punching, and all he saw before him was —

All hell breaking loose.

An irrigation ditch.

Dig in!

Christ, captain, where are they all coming from?

The question all but lost beneath a cacophony of mortar fire, static from the radio, the whine of rocket-propelled grenades —

Hell breaking loose . . .

And then, in rapid succession, the names of the fallen — of Richards and Poole, Nelson and Crane, Griffin, Bellaver, Muñoz, Dunn —

But this time there was something else in there, too, something that wasn't usually part of this memory — a voice, a woman's voice, calling a name —

'Max! Max, stop it! You're killing him!'

Max?

Who the hell is Max?

You're Max . . .

He realized suddenly that the girl was trying to drag him off the Taliban leader they'd come here to capture or kill. Maybe she was one of his wives.

Except . . .

Except that the man beneath him *wasn't* a Taliban leader.

Oh God, oh Christ, it's a civilian . . .

No — it's Nicky.

And finally, there it was; the hook by which he was able to draw himself back from the past.

One more punch would do it, knock Nicky from this life into the next, and he was a fraction of a heartbeat away from delivering it.

But instead he held back, forced himself to see —

— a winter scene, with snowflakes drifting slowly, silently to earth —

— a tropical island paradise with a resplendent magenta sunset dropping over a golden blue ocean —

— a scene from *A Day at the Races;* Groucho Marx taking someone's pulse and saying: 'Either he's dead or my watch has stopped.'

He fell sideways off Nicky and started sucking in air. He was back, it was over.

It was *over* . . .

And *Nicky* was over, too; finished.

Nicky . . . now living on borrowed time.

Max tried to sit up, got as far as one elbow, looked at the mess he'd made of Nicky and felt nothing, no revulsion, no pride.

Then Kate was kneeling over him, holding him, hugging him, crying and laughing and just relieved to have him back, to have him *not* be the man who killed Nicky Crocetti.

He gave one final shudder, then tried to form his battered mouth into a grin. 'I didn't kill her,' he managed.

'What?'

'Diana,' he said, and cleared his throat. 'I didn't kill her. It was Aaron.'

'Aaron?'

'Aaron, all along.'

'Can you prove it?' she asked urgently.

He thought about Elizabeth, and nodded.

'Then it's over,' she said.

'For them,' he told her, meaning Aaron and Nicky.

'But not for us,' she said hopefully.

'For us,' he said, and carefully put his aching arms around her, 'this is just the beginning.'

24

Christopher Callan, muffled against the chilly November air, looked out over the sea of graves before him, each one marking the final resting place of a man or woman who had paid the ultimate price for protecting their country, and drew a soft breath.

Out there lay Richards and Pool, Nelson and Crane, Griffin, Bellaver, Muñoz and Dunn.

But things were different for him now; better. It no longer mattered if some people might still thought he'd run out on them that day in Afghanistan. He knew that he hadn't. And more importantly, *they* knew it, too. And that was all that really mattered.

He understood that now.

And with that understanding, with the right counseling and the knowledge that he hadn't after all murdered his wife, a curious calming effect had come upon him and gradually helped him overcome the violence within him, and conquer the blackouts that had always accompanied it.

As he stood here now, paying his respects to the war dead, he had been free of the blackouts for almost three whole months.

He allowed himself to stare out across the headstones one final time, then brought his right arm up in a sharp, textbook salute.

He held the salute for ten long seconds, standing there with his back straight and his shoulders squared and his jaw tilted proudly high. Then his arm dropped back to his side and he turned and made his way back to his car — the car he drove now that he was no longer saddled with the Civic.

Kate and Melanie stood beside the vehicle, waiting for him to join them, their breath steaming in the crisp autumn sunshine.

At the sight of them Chris Callan felt himself smiling again. It seemed he'd done a lot of that recently. And his smile turned to a broad grin as he went to join them.

We do hope that you have enjoyed reading this large print book.

Did you know that all of our titles are available for purchase?

We publish a wide range of high quality large print books including:

Romances, Mysteries, Classics
General Fiction
Non Fiction and Westerns

Special interest titles available in large print are:

The Little Oxford Dictionary
Music Book, Song Book
Hymn Book, Service Book

Also available from us courtesy of Oxford University Press:

Young Readers' Dictionary
(large print edition)
Young Readers' Thesaurus
(large print edition)

For further information or a free brochure, please contact us at:
Ulverscroft Large Print Books Ltd.,
The Green, Bradgate Road, Anstey,
Leicester, LE7 7FU, England.
Tel: (00 44) **0116 236 4325**
Fax: (00 44) **0116 234 0205**

THE ANGEL

Gerald Verner

For months, Scotland Yard was interested in the mysterious Angela Kesson, who they dubbed 'the Angel', with her striking beauty. Her male acquaintances had dubious reputations. And in every instance, at the start of each relationship, their homes were burgled and money and valuables stolen. Though unemployed, she lived in an expensive flat, but there was insufficient proof for an arrest. However when her latest escort's home was burgled — he had been murdered, his head crushed like an eggshell . . .

THE TRIALS OF QUINTILIAN

Michael Kurland

In ancient Rome, Marcus Fabius Quintilianus was a real barrister, honoured for being a teacher, rhetorician, jurist and a crime solver . . . In these three stories Quintilian, a character who is based on this early detective, chronicles some of the eminent man's cases. The opening tale, set in the last half of the first century AD, is 'Blind Justice' — where Quintilian must defend a blind man accused of brutal patricide . . .

DEATH SET IN DIAMONDS

Gerald Verner

On a golfing holiday, playwright and criminologist Trevor Lowe and his assistant are on their way to see Sir Reginald Allerdyce. They encounter an old friend, Detective-Inspector Shadgold, investigating a criminal known as the diamond bandit and three robberies committed in four weeks — all involving diamonds. When Lowe discovers that Sir Reginald has been murdered, he suddenly becomes involved in the case. So begins a chain of events that plunges all three of them into deadly danger . . .

THE MAN WHO STOPPED THE DUST

John Russell Fearn

Professor Renhard dies accidentally whilst experimenting with a machine that destroys dust. Meanwhile, when Dr. Anderson operates on a young woman, an accidental slip of the surgeon's knife leads to more than her death. The girl's brother, Gaston — Renhard's manservant — festers with revenge and incriminates Anderson, who is eventually judged as certified insane. When he is then incarcerated in an asylum, Gaston's revenge is complete. However — only Dr. Anderson could avert the catastrophic consequences of Renhard's mad experiments . . .

BACK TO THE LEGION

Gordon Landsborough

The Brotherhood of Tormented Men is comprised of individuals who were prisoners, tortured in the underground cells of secret police in a dozen Arab countries. On a mission, they have crossed continents to rendezvous in the middle of the Sahara. When a travel-stained group of ex-legionnaires comes upon them, that mission should spell death to the men of the Foreign Legion. But death comes to men who accept it, and these legionnaires are fighters who refuse to accept death . . .

ONLY THE RUTHLESS CAN PLAY

John Burke

In the city of London, the *Career Development Functions* rooms are situated on the tenth floor of International Synthetics. There, people undergo the 'Fifth Executive Course'. The participants expect a gruelling challenge — one in which men fight for power — knowing that the going will be tough. But they don't expect one of their members to die in gruesome circumstances. So, is this a test of their reactions — or the insane ambitions of one of their own number?